Administrator

1974

Administrator

Mayumura Taku

translated by
Daniel Jackson

KURODAHAN PRESS 2004

Originally published in Japan as *Shiseikan* by Hayakawa Shobō, Tokyo

Copyright © 1974 by Mayumura Taku

English translation copyright © 2004 by Daniel Jackson

This edition © 2004 by Kurodahan Press

FG-J0001-L1

ISBN 4-902075-00-8

KURODAHAN PRESS

EDWARD LIPSETT · STEPHEN A. CARTER · CHRIS RYAL

KURODAHAN PRESS IS A DIVISION OF INTERCOM LTD.

#403 TENJIN 3-9-10, CHUO-KU, FUKUOKA 810-0001 JAPAN

Administrator

The Flame and the Blossom

— I —

HE WONDERED AGAIN why he was so moved by the sight. From the first time he had seen it, it had always moved him. It always perturbed him: that strangely plaintive spectacle, strangely bald, for all its brilliance. He could feel something awaken and cry out deep inside him, desolately. Each time it did, he would be perplexed, at a loss for how to control it.

To be more precise, it had changed from when he first saw it. It now was more wrenching – he was more biased, and he realized that change now.

Maybe it was because of Amilla.

The fact that it was Amilla's kin covering the dome of the sky, pressing across it, was twisting the balance of his judgment.

How he felt about them: who showed such reason, who were symbolized to him by Amilla – finally unable to resist the demands of instinct and dancing up into the sky…

No.

Wasn't he merely jealous?

Countless bits of colored confetti were floating in the sunset sky. These strangely shaped beings rode the powerful seasonal winds that blew once a year – by human standards, once every four months – floating up into the air, spreading, filling in the sky with color, and drifting. Flowers, two or three meters in diameter. Changing colors every few seconds, red and yellow and purple, all the possible hues, flowing through the sky like the legendary locust swarms of Terra, on their great mating journey.

It made an awesome harmony all together. When that group over there was yellow, the ones over his head would flash pure white, and those thousands in the distance shone a blue deeper than the sky – the endlessly covered sky was a variegated pattern, flowing away to the horizon, ever to the horizon. This year, it had started this afternoon, their numbers growing rapidly, through this sunset, through the night, through dawn… As long as the fierce seasonal wind continued… The great hordes that would persevere as long as the wind lasted, even if he didn't like it... On their great reproductive flight.

To them, whether this "floating" was a liberation or an end, whether it was an act of suffering or in the realm of love – as a Terran, he didn't know. He had to admit that it was like entrusting your body to the summoning voices of your kind, a being that had come from the distant past. He had to admit it marked a phase of their existence as reasoning beings.

How would he feel then?

Amilla, too, would finally drift in the sky like that, and what would he think then?

Was he jealous? He searched his heart again. Even though those were Amilla's kin, Amilla wasn't with them this time. He told himself Amilla wasn't there this time, but still... Amilla would be, someday, and he was upset by merely thinking that it was the normal manner of reproduction for Amilla. That thought showed him how much it had affected him, and though he understood, there was no helping it.

Still.

The degree to which he had let it affect him... Wasn't it inevitable, really? Didn't all of his life, before he was officially installed as Administrator, force him to become this way?

Right.

He had to admit that he had such a weak point in him.

A fault.

And that fault was the reverse side of attaining the position of Administrator. In his same class, there were no doubt happy ones who never realized it, and others who were able to overcome the problem easily.

But he wasn't one of them. He, Kurobe PPK Taiji, wasn't such a person.

Of course, he had been selected out as a candidate for Administrator and had been sent here after training upon training, over ten years of concentrated study. Mentally and physically, he had been forged into a member of the elite. Naturally, he felt the contradiction in that. As much as he thought of his "eliteness", he thought of it as a strenuous process that he had invested himself in, with his elite status as the end result.

4

Thinking like his would never produce so common a result as looking over his own shoulder into the past. He and his group were many hundreds of times more competitive than the masses who merely inhabited Terra. They were still unquestionably in the highest group, even when compared to the judges, so strictly selected, or – to go to the other extreme – the space service men, who were at the very summit of the reflexes and senses.

Still, his had been a selection process made with the deletion of emotions as a prerequisite. There was a basis to the quiet whispers of condemnation and complaint against him and his kind throughout Terra and Terran space. That was because theoretical and multi-objective training were thought to be essential in the training of an Administrator, and that idea was put into practice.

But was it really possible to delete the emotions?

In spite of that oath at the beginning of their training, many candidates, possibly even possessed of outstanding political capabilities, were unable to withstand the sympathetic vibrations of their emotions, lost their balance, and failed. He had managed somehow to finish the entire process without running, and received his post, but you couldn't say he had no emotions at all. He had simply frozen his yearnings, and was inviting disruption by always putting it off until later, until later. It only supported him.

Yearnings?

No, wasn't it better to change that to desires? And infantile desires, at that...

Right.

For example, what was this strangeness deep in his heart? Was it really anything more than mere illusion?

He thought.

He thought about what his strangeness was.

Mmm...

A very wise, innocent, lovable, too-knowing little girl. A girl that used her cunning only for a man, for the man she loved. A girl with a good, clear head, who was solitary though everyone knew her. A young woman come like an angel, a sprite, like a shadow, her life full of the ups and downs of men. Weak courage, strong will, a nobility that encompasses the anger of the masses...

Where was that person? Not likely to be anywhere. That kind of woman existed only in the mind, was made to suit the reader as the heroine of a story. Even though he knew that, he couldn't rid himself of the image – and believing that she would appear somewhere, someday, had only convinced him more firmly.

What could he call it except infantile illusion?

Wasn't he hoping deep in his heart that he could fulfill that desire somewhere in Terran space, if not on Terra itself? And could he stay as he was without exploding?

Frankly, there were times when he wondered if those who trained the candidates didn't make full use of these illusions.

There was no mistake that this repressed longing, this never-to-be-realized hope, had erupted when he came to live on this different world. Hadn't that eruption fused too brightly with the principle that long-term administration was impossible without a strong connection with the native inhabitants? While claiming it as a necessary action for the performance of his duty, hadn't he tread this path to its inevitable end?

No... Stop it.

It was no use attacking himself like that. It would only make his heart heavier the more he berated himself. Luckily, no one else had noticed that psychological bent in him. Yet. And even if someone did, he had done nothing reprehensible.

I wonder when... he asked himself. *I wonder when this started...*

— 2 —

"The seasonal winds will begin soon, Administrator," said SQI.

"Uh-huh." Kurobe lifted his head.

"The seasonal winds," repeated SQI, the chief of all the robots scattered about the planet, its stainless steel face turned fixedly to the sky. "In about ten days or so, the seasonal winds will blow, and the flowering native inhabitants will rise up into the sky. If we are going to control their landing zones, we must begin preparations at once. Will you give permission to begin operations?"

Kurobe shook his head slightly. "No. Permission denied."

"For what reason?"

"Because there is no need for it."

"Such control has always been exercised up until now. The spermatozoa will wait where they land, and then reproduce without order. We cannot protect and raise them all with our limited materials and capacity. As a result the wild native population will increase dramatically. Is that acceptable?"

"That's OK."

"Why? During the previous seasonal winds, we applied control. At that time, weren't you already in full command here as Administrator?"

"I was here, and I'd already taken over command, but it's going to be different from now on."

"Would you explain why?"

"I though I'd already explained, in general. Well, it doesn't matter. Any detailed directive has to be explained... In the past it was best to do as you said. That was the 'war preparatory stance' – in other words, Class II. However, that is over now. The Federation is putting a new governing method into practice, and this world has been redesignated as Class III, Type B... I said all this before, right?"

"Yes, I heard that one hundred and eight hours ago," said SQI expressionlessly. "Still, as I said at that time, I don't understand the use of the word Class."

7

"I know. That's because it's a new concept, which accompanied the change in the policy of colonial government. Of course it is not in your memory banks. Well, this idea was around long ago, too, but I imagine it was only made into official policy recently. At any rate, a detailed explanation has arrived, and if you'll go to the library and read it you'll understand."

"I will do so."

"If you read it, you'll understand easily – but to sum it up, a 'Class III, Type B' designation means allowing the world concerned to revert to its original condition as much as possible, to maintain a policy of minimum interference. That's why we won't easily interfere any more. If the winds blow, let them blow. If the flowers fly, let them. OK?"

The robot didn't answer immediately. After a pause, it said "After I verify the documents, I will follow your directive."

After it replied, SQI turned its four wheels and left the room.

A bitter smile floated on Kurobe's face as he watched it leave.

Just like a stubborn old man.

Of course, that didn't mean the robot was stupid or bad. For the express purpose of controlling possible excesses by Administrators, the robots were intentionally built to be unable to accept new orders without going through the proper procedures, and they were unable to erase previous orders. An application of the principle of inertia. That's why SQI was so irritatingly methodical, even to Kurobe. And it was true that there was a real danger in having the robots changing the color of government policies like a chameleon at the Administrator's whim. It would cause misunderstanding and friction between the native inhabitants and the various local bureaus... And Kurobe was unable to deny that such Administrators did currently exist, or that they might appear in the future. Still, there was no mistake that the many Administrators installed on various worlds were not happy about their robots' sulky attitudes.

Even so, you couldn't say the robots were a loss to the Administrators, or only a nuisance. Quite the opposite. As groups of specialists on the various worlds, the robots were an absolute necessity for government.

They functioned as superb teams, always fulfilling their duties. The only problem was how well that new type of government, the Administrator system, could utilize those abilities.

It was night when he finished his work.

He had to retire to his room and rest. He just couldn't seem to adjust to this twenty-hour day, but it felt like he had finally grasped the tempo instead of being pushed along by it.

As he stood, the blinking of the desk light caught his eye.

A communication was coming in.

He picked it up.

It was a message from the commander of the patrol that covered System 925 – including this world, Sarulunin – asking to come and meet with him in the near future. The patrol base for System 925 was located on the next planet out, and if he chose to come here he could do so easily. This commander, though, was a little young, and put work first, and so always gave a few days notice before his visits.

Kurobe fed the communication into his "Handle" box. Now the robots would go to meet him, and make all the preparations.

He entered the small elevator in the Administrator's Office, and rode down.

I wonder what in the world the commander wants to talk about, he thought. After meeting the commander one or two times, he knew he wasn't likely to come for an enjoyable chat. He was an officer acutely conscious of his responsibilities, and all too aware of his own authority. If he took the trouble to come and meet him, he must really have something to talk about.

Was he going to come pressing another demand?

Naturally, it was legally acceptable to ignore those demands. There was absolutely no need for the Administrator of this world, who held total responsibility, to worry about the demands of a mere system commander. No need, but... Behind the patrol were the Federation Forces, and regardless of the reason, it would be awkward to get in the way of the Forces.

That commander hadn't forgotten that all colonial worlds had been under military rule. He didn't think very much of this strange new breed of "Administrators" that had stolen all of the rights of government... That wasn't quite accurate. The Administrators had been cultivated under Federation policy, and represented only a change in authority; but to the Forces, that seemed to mean theft.

And also – Kurobe shrugged his shoulders in the cramped elevator and gave a laugh – wasn't that commander forgetting that even if Sarulunin was put under military rule again, he wasn't likely to be the person with the authority? Leaving aside such things as environment, the presence or absence of native inhabitants, colonial conditions and whatever natural resources might be available, the number of planets still under Forces control, as before, was much greater than the few that had been transferred to the Administrators... In any case, the person at the top, or the person who had been at the top, was the Sector Administrator, or another of the same rank. Here on Sarulunin, Kalgeist had been in command before Kurobe took over, the same Kalgeist who was so famous for his merciless conquest of new systems. That was the standard, and it wasn't likely that a mere commander-class officer with maybe a dozen ships would ever get his chance. In spite of that, for the commander to brazenly come here and make demands in the guise of opinion made Kurobe think that he just had too much faith in his own position as commander... Or, maybe, had he been installed as the successor to Kalgeist?

The elevator door opened.

A metallic clink. With that, the defense of the Administrator shifted over from LQ3's command to LQ4's.

A section of the floor rose to become a seat, and he sat down. The corridor began to move him towards his room.

There seemed to be no irregularity in the construction of the robots. Even when there was, it was fixed before he even noticed, 99.99% of the time – fixed for the Administrator.

No, not just the Administrator. For the supreme authority of this world, whoever it might be. Before he had come, all this had been for Kalgeist.

Kalgeist.

Kurobe recalled the last night he had talked with Kalgeist.

"No doubt about it: the worlds – or rather, the very essence of the Federation – is changing," muttered Kalgeist, taking a sip from his glass.

Yet there was almost no dissatisfaction or anger in his voice as he said it. That was probably because Kalgeist himself could retire before it damaged his glorious reputation, and because he could claim, truthfully, that the cause of his withdrawal was the passage of time, not a cowardly urge for self-preservation. In that sense, to Kurobe, he looked like not Cortez or Patton, but rather an old acclaimed lion, or a noble wolf… Still, sometimes he growled unexpectedly, surprising Kurobe, baring his fangs through the fabric of age. "Well, I guess it's only reasonable it should change."

The liquor undoubtedly helped, but Kalgeist's eyes were looking at something very far away.

"The Federation has expanded and expanded for a hundred years. There was no choice but to continue. The Federation tried to destroy its internal contradictions and congestion by turning them to the outside. It evolved always thinking: 'What new planet will be discovered? How can we make it valuable to us? Can we expect a colony there?' It was the roughest, fastest way; but people such as myself understand that there was no better way."

He took a breath.

"But that's reached its limit now. New generations succeed old, and that rash expansionist policy has at last come to an end. Terrans have come to think that they are always the nobility on new planets, and then they lose their surprise, their self-consciousness. Mm… the third, the fourth colonial worlds still had their uniqueness when the thirtieth and fortieth were added, but now we don't want that. Not now, when the settlers have come to be vocal about the system citizenship they claim."

Unusually talkative. The drink must have loosened his tongue, and the talking made him more drunk.

"The total is zero."

Kalgeist nodded deeply two or three times. "The effect of the limitation on the conquest of new worlds is zero, no, even negative. When the age of starflight technology reached the point where it changed from revolutionary principles to minor improvements, the expansion fell a notch – and the age when the center of the sphere was more important than the periphery arrived. Humanity is now shut in a greenhouse. The policy of the Federation has undergone a massive reversal."

Kalgeist fell silent.

Kurobe waited patiently. He had heard all this before, and he didn't want to listen to it again. Still, it would be against etiquette, even a little arrogant, to show he was not listening (especially to someone like Kalgeist). It was a ritual to him.

"Human-ruled space is changing in character."

He said exactly what Kurobe had expected.

"Like the entrance on the scene of you Administrators. They say you're the political rulers for single worlds. I guess since the Federation raised you for that purpose it's not just a joke, but... People like me can't help but think the Administrator system is a little suspicious."

"I think I understand what you want to say."

"Understand? Listen to you! This isn't something you understand! You either feel it or you don't. It's not anything you can *understand*." Kalgeist grew angry for an instant, then it cleared away.

"You people say governing is a science. Maybe it's just parroting hollow-headed Federation thinking, but anyway, you believe it. Governing is a finely-calculated technique, you say. But if you give us our say, it's different. Government, at the very basic level, is what marks the relationship between the killers and the killed, the rulers and the ruled. It's no comedy. It's something that was born on a tightrope between *overcome* and *be overcome*. Bluntly, what the person at the top needs is not compromise or intelligence. It's the ability to decide, and the authority to enforce the decision. Understand?! Hell, you're not likely to understand, are you?"

"..." Kurobe only smiled, slightly.

"I've killed a goodly number of natives on a good many worlds." Maybe Kurobe's lack of response added heat to the fire, but Kalgeist raised his voice a notch.

"I felt it was a pity about the dead. No, maybe I didn't. To us, they are always the enemy. Well, in any case, you people who castigate our actions are indulgent, lukewarm over-conceited idiots. War and conquest *are* that way. Looking on those who have to do the dirty work as heretics, saying you didn't dirty your hands, isn't that a little vain? Right? And even those actions, if you take the long view, were for the peace and well-being of the majority of those natives. Without conquest, how can you hope to guide those lesser than us? Eventually, you have to admit we did what we had to do."

Kurobe thought that it was the same one-sided theory as always.

Kurobe could certainly have put up a serious attempt at a counter-theory to Kalgeist's; but even if he did, Kalgeist would certainly not change his thinking, and Kurobe had too much awareness of his own duty to violate this ritual. It was better to listen silently now, and then put his own ideas into effect when he became Administrator. Of course, Kalgeist was a hero of the past. It was polite and formal to bury him now, without getting involved.

"Still, that philosophy is no longer accepted in the Federation, it seems," said Kalgeist, gazing into space. "They're all good people who don't even stop to consider what it is that supports them. Those oh-so-good souls at the Federation have forgotten, and now solve nothing by force, saying that military rule causes more damage to our own side. And they say it seriously. That this is an era when things will be taken over by a consummately trained elite."

He trained his eyes on Kurobe and continued.

"Under special circumstances, I guess even this is possible. In nice stable lukewarm water, I guess they can govern through you. Reduce the story down to just planetary government, and maybe the era has come where you can handle it with the power of your robots. But what'll you do when things get dangerous? And I'll tell you now, rebellions have always cropped up in human history, and leaders always emerge. You are just a filler, a link, until that happens. Mm... You are only useful if order, the present order, is maintained. For example, if a race as advanced as humans appeared and came attacking, you would be useless. Just because it hasn't happened yet, you can't say it won't happen. And what'll you do then? All of your government by rules, your techniques, will disappear. You will vanish from history, yielding your seats to people with real government, real power. Not that it matters a damn to me whether you vanish or whatever... But if the transfer of power doesn't go smoothly, then what? Maybe humanity will vanish. Have you considered that? And if you haven't, isn't that gambling with the fate of humanity without insurance? You intelligentsia should have thought of it, I know. But you are the systematized elite, and the systematized elite can never forget that it is impossible to overcome your own era."

That's true, though Kurobe. And as he thought it, he realized that the Administrator was needed at this point in time. Even as a temporary relief measure, Administrators could help the Federation.

"Well," said Kalgeist, getting up unsteadily, "Sorry to get it all off my chest like that. Me, I've seen many worlds where there's never been a human footprint before. I've met animals, beings, totally different from humanity in their thinking processes. That's why I can imagine a hell of a lot more 'what ifs' than you cloistered Administrators."

He gave a low laugh.

"Also, one of my grandsons is studying to be your junior – he's learning 'Administratoring'. When he told me, I was furious and ordered him to stop, but of course he didn't listen, and entered the Academy anyway. It looks like I told you what I wanted to tell him. Anyway... Think of it that way, will you?"

Kalgeist raised a hand vaguely, and left the room. Kurobe thought he was just a little too drunk for a man who had to attend another party that night.

Trying to suppress and erase that scene reborn in memory, he slid into his private room. Wryly, he thought to himself that military men were like that... The patrol commander, too, was the same – no, the same breed but on a lower level.

But that recollection held such a true-to-life quality he was stunned. Probably, the reality of meals without company, of taking over all that solitary investigation and probing, of sleeping alone – again, repeated again and again – had made it feel so. Directing machines, surrounded by machines, wouldn't he become as stale and old as the machines themselves? Exactly because he was an Administrator, supported by all those techniques, didn't he lack the ability to adapt? Weren't the Administrators, in other words, nothing more than an evanescent elite? Maybe Kalgeist had been right... He couldn't help but feel that way.

And, within it all, what was he? What did he possess? When his precious techniques couldn't cope, when the effect of his manipulations vanished, what could he be?

Wasn't he nothing?

Something... Was there at least something he whole-heartedly pursued?

Nothing.

Suddenly, he thought he wanted something. He thought he wanted something to drive him that would bubble up from inside himself, not orders and skills imparted to the Administrator from the outside. And if it was possible, to meld it with his sense of purpose as an Administrator. It had to exist somewhere...

He was asking for the impossible. It couldn't be.

He pressed his lips together, and reached his arm out to press the switch for dinner.

Had it started then? Had his inclination towards that *something* started then, in that instant?

When he looked up, the sky was past sunset. The countless flowers drifted across the heavens in a flow of colored phosphorescence.

He looked away from the flowers and gave a heavy sigh.

Or, maybe...

"Will you be going out?" asked LQ3's wall-mount contact, after he pushed the button.

"Mmm. Regular observation," he answered, but of course the door didn't open immediately. The restless robots were communicating. LQ3 would report to SQ1, which would, after verifying the situation, pass an order down to the attendant chief, SQ2, which would, in turn, order SQQ4 and SQQ5 to make preparations while ordering LQ2's group to take over protection of the Administrator. After all of these preparations were finished, and SQ1 had checked with all sections, including observation, and received acknowledgement, it would finally order SQ3 to open to door.

In less than a minute, the door opened, and Kurobe slid down the chute to the ground.

The car was waiting.

Not just one. In all, there were eight cars, but only three of them were usable by humans: the Administrator's car, which also carried SQ2, and the two spares. The others were attendants.

In the lead was the LQQ7 combat tank, then the LQQ8 protective screen unit, and the communications/scout LQQ9 unit. The light assault types LQX3 and LQX4 surrounded his vehicle. Even this was a small-scale force, as this was a regularly scheduled observation. For a trip to the main centers of Sarulunin, over forty ground and air vehicles were fielded, under the direct control of SQ1.

When he settled down in his seat in the central car, he gave the order.

"Pass between the east cluster of colonies, to the First Research Station, and then return. However, immediately after my discussion at the research station, we must return by a roundabout route."

The order was verified by SQ2, and then transferred to LQ2, and to the entire fleet. Immediately the armored column began to advance over the rough rocky terrain at forty kilometers per hour.

In all probability, people like Kalgeist never thought in detail about the formation of these robots. To Kalgeist and his ilk, if robots were merely useful, that was enough. They would say that even though robots, which were capable of communicating by means impossible for humans, were useful, they had no inherent meaning. But Kurobe, as a trained professional, knew their capabilities, and knew how they would react to particular commands. It seemed like a minor thing, but it was a highly important difference.

When he met the patrol commander, it was always that way.

He recalled the times they had spoken together, and a deprecating smile came to his lips.

Kurobe already knew well that the patrol commander for System 925 was stubborn behind all hope.

He wasn't entirely happy about him – Thompson – coming here when the system was classified as Class III, Type B, and seeing if that amateur (yes, he used that word) Administrator was loyally following the instructions of the Federation.

Thompson had been here twice before this seasonal wind. And three times before that... And before that... And Kurobe knew what he would say, and he always repeated the same things.

Administrator, what are you doing? Is this what you call government? Leaving this planet wild and uncontrolled is totally irresponsible. Isn't this a colony world for the use of humanity? Why doesn't the Federation say something? Anything?... The only planet in this system with a breathable atmosphere is Sarulunin. Why should we have to squeeze air and water out of rocks for our patrol base? And leave this planet to those vegetable monsters? How about if you gave us a nice big area here to patrol? We like hunting here. Shooting vegetables is good for our psychological hygiene. You should be able to give us at least that. After all, the military took this planet in the first place... And so on. And so on.

He never ended, just on and on. In response, Kurobe merely refused: sometimes politely, and sometimes as a hard-and-fast rule. Thompson would grow exasperated, and show only his desire to take what he wanted. The men and robots he brought with him learned from that. If there was ever trouble on this frontier world from the outside, it was probable he would be in deep trouble because of military pressure.

The only thing guaranteeing Kurobe's safety was the robots – or rather, his knowledge of robots. He knew exactly what situations the robots would judge as dangerous, exactly how to make them activate their recording devices, exactly what orders to give to avoid being falsely accused of something or killed, and would always take the appropriate counter-measures in advance.

At some point in time, that patrol commander would notice Kurobe's weak point, his distrust of Administrators would flare up, and he would light a fire under Kurobe by filing a complaint with his superiors. Still, until now Kurobe had showed no gap in his defenses, and he didn't plan to show any. He wasn't such a fool as to be tripped up by anyone like Thompson. He had the knowledge and the training to avoid it.

…He frowned.

That's strange, he thought.

That I should be telling myself how superior I am… I must have some serious doubts, he thought to himself. Am I so scared of something that I use self-intoxication to avoid looking it in the face?

The car caravan passed over the rocky belt where the Administration Complex was located, and continued to the level plain.

There was no ocean – at least, not as he thought of the word. Although Sarulunin had shallow lakes, it didn't have anything that could be called an ocean – and, as a result, except for the scattered low outcrops, the entire planet was a giant marsh. The work of erosion had almost finished, and the next mountain-building movement wouldn't start for some time. Though there would be one in the future, the result of the past and present stress investigation showed that this was a much more tranquil planet than Terra.

Which was certainly not to say that this was a silent, sleeping world. Even thought it was marshy, under its sun's fierce rays it could become parched, and as Sarulunin's axial tilt was almost thirty degrees, the seasonal changes were violent. The ground released all its moisture around the tropics, and for the first few days of autumn the seasonal winds blew.

Another thing that gave a special character to this world was its incredibly fecund vegetation. Maybe because it was so close to a к-type star and received more radiation than Terra, there were many strange varieties of plants, all locked in a fierce competition for survival. No animals were here, but the explanation did not lie in the fact that there was no ocean to spawn them. Rather, it seemed that they had been rendered extinct by the plants, which had developed in remarkable forms and could move like animals themselves.

Kurobe's car moved forward on caterpillar tracks, crushing the grass, spraying water and mud. That grass wasn't sentient, and would only become the food of higher organisms, so there was no problem here at all.

If a brownish or yellowish growth appeared, through, the caravan would carefully steer around it. Those were the low-level Sarulunia: individuals separated from their home-trees, meandering about to gather grass as fodder and to defend their home-tree's territory. They didn't have all that much intelligence, but some of them were unbelievably ferocious, and when they saw something moving they would rustle their tendrils like a centipede and come rushing to the attack.

That wasn't all they had to be careful of. The column led by sq2 also avoided the muddy pools in the marsh that were visible here and there. One meter of water or mud was no problem for the physical capabilities of the cars, but living in that muddy water were the larvae of the low- and high-level Sarulunia, and if they accidentally trod on one, they would be instantly attacked.

Still, this was slightly north of the sub-tropic zone, so the cars could at least move. In the tropical rain forests it was pandemonium, never knowing what monsters would appear; of course, unarmored humans were helpless, and even carefully designed robots sometimes failed to return.

After about two hours of traveling through the continuous rain, they reached an area where the vegetation became increasingly ordered, and grouped together by type.

Large dark-green hemispheres began to be visible here and there. The area around each dome was bare earth. Pink, bumpy, drum-shaped beings one hundred to one hundred fifty centimeters in height were working around or entering and leaving the dwelling, on their dozen or so roots that served as tentacles. This was a colony of true Sarulunia.

"It's a little tough, because it's only been a little over ten years since the planet was discovered. Well, I guess it's a good chance to show off your ability as an Administrator... In any case, the local researchers will tell you the details about the Sarulunia. I'll just cover the basic facts now."

The upper-grade information officer of the Ministry of Space Development sat down in front of Kurobe, who was looking at the 3D photographs, and began his explanation. "I think you've already noticed, but the name 'Sarulunia' was freely adapted by us from the name of the planet. It's not what they call themselves. They have their own names... It's just not possible for us to duplicate their pronunciation, as it's made by releasing water vapor. Plus which, since we've got the translator machine, it's enough to merely call them Sarulunia."

"Please continue," pressed Kurobe.

"Mm. Well, anyway, these Sarulunia are now almost definitely the highest form of intelligent life on Sarulunin. The low-level Sarulunin are at about level two or three."

"About the same as dogs or horses. And how about the level of the higher types – the true Sarulunia?"

"That's very unclear," said the information officer, shrugging his shoulders. "The researchers say it varies. Whether that's caused by lack of co-operation from the true Sarulunia, or by large differences between individuals, is unclear... In any case, they are not the livestock-class animals that Kalgeist and his underlings thought. Kalgeist made that assessment offhand, just from the structure of their domes. At the same time, though, there is the example of the jellyfish of Ross 780 II, the main inhabitants of Kirielin, which were found to have a high capacity for thought and communication even without any material culture... Well, our methods of evaluating different cultures aren't very developed yet, so it should be left to the Administrator on the spot."

"... I see."

"I thought you would. Anyway, to continue, reproduction on Sarulunin is a little different than ours." The officer took out some material. "If you look at this illustration, you'll understand in general, but I'll go over it. Usually, the spermatozoa larvae, looking something like an insect, fertilizes the flower by crawling in. Of course, the flowers are different depending on the type of Sarulunia. The true Sarulunia are very odd, and actually fly on the seasonal winds, but the basic pattern is the same."

"Mmm..."

"This fertilization is undoubtedly for the protection of the species. Before birth, it is common to divide many times. In other words: one egg, many offspring; so that over one hundred individuals can be born with the same genetic pattern. These burrow into the wet ground, and after they grow and develop locomotive tendrils, they set off on their journey, devouring low-level plants as they go."

"Journey?"

"Journey. The details aren't understood very well yet, but they have the urge to return to the home colony that spawned them, even when young, on an instinctual level. Of course, they have many natural enemies, so over half of them are eaten on the way. Even so, they keep trying. At the same time, they strive to replace their numbers through sexless reproduction. Really, a heart-rending tale."

"And then?"

"The young ones have very little time. They must reach their colony before the onset of the next dry season. If they don't make it, their skin loses its moisture, changes substance, and their tendrils become articulated. They become, in other words, spermatozoa larvae. Failed young Sarulunia become larva, and produce sperm, and are fated to find a flower the next mating season, or the one after that."

He tapped the photograph Kurobe was holding. "Most of them become larvae. Only the most fortunate make the trip in time."

"…"

"Among the ones that can't return in time, there are some that try to enter other colonies by force. With the low-level Sarulunia, there is no problem, but not so with the true Sarulunia. The colony's individuals make decisions about whether to admit a young one or not based on the arrival rate and the genetic pattern of that particular young."

He breathed out heavily.

"The ones that are allowed in, and the ones that are admitted naturally because they started there, connect their tendrils to the home-tree, and grow for two or three seasons as a part of it. That's when they become true Sarulunia."

"…"

"While they are developing as parts of the home-tree, they are endowed with intelligence, knowledge, and senses by it. At the proper time, they separate, and move on their own… as motile Sarulunia."

The information officer leaned back in his chair, and laced his hands together. "As for the Sarulunia motiles – well, maybe they shouldn't be called plants. They come and go as they like, and eat lesser vegetation. They receive their water from the home-tree, but other than that, they live by plunder. They live off other vegetation. They can assimilate the material they collect, and have very well developed sense organs. And, because they have no chlorophyll for photosynthesis, they breathe – and very powerfully."

"A highly distinctive life form."

"Exactly. If you go by previous experience. To us, it's easier to understand silicon-based life forms. Still, there are scholars who say it's much easier if you just think of the motile Sarulunia as an alternate bud form."

"A bud."

"Yes. Most of those motiles flower after one year – in other words, after four Terran months. Only the true Sarulunia are different. The true Sarulunia can willfully control their flowering, put it off until the next season. And not just the next season. They can keep putting it off, from season to season. They can remain motiles as long as they will it. In this way, they have succeeded in co-operatively raising the intelligence level of their colonies. Just as the reason we humans first used both hands and made fire is unclear, it's not clear why they did this, but it is the decisive difference between low-level and true Sarulunia. To the latter, return to the home-tree and abandonment of all movement rapidly leads to loss of intelligence. You could say that the true Sarulunia emerged as this world's prime contender by extending their intelligent period."

"Wait a minute," Kurobe broke in. "Doesn't that mean that the true Sarulunia are gradually becoming extinct? The number of motiles increases while the number of flowers decreases."

The information officer smiled. "No. No, not quite... It's not that way. The reason is that all of the motiles opt to become flowers after a number of seasons."

He stared into space, and spoke in a murmur. "Of course, I've never seen the real thing... The flowers floating on the seasonal winds. I've seen a 3D movie of it, once... It had grandeur. A glorious, splendid sight..."

He had seen that flight now three times.

He understood what the information officer couldn't, and had experienced here what he could never have experienced back on Terra.

For example, although the true Sarulunia were the representative intelligent life form on this world, they were also very weak in the higher latitudes, and their territory was continuously invaded by the ferocious plants from the tropical rain forests... He knew now that they weren't just collections of home-trees, but rather that they were divided into central and branch home-trees, and that each domain was determined by the number of motiles and their power and so on, and that at times there was intense war... Since he had come here, he had been taught by the researchers, had seen with his own eyes, and had finally understood.

And he had also had the strange experience of exchanging thoughts with the true Sarulunia through the translator every time he came. To express the thoughts of Terrans to the native inhabitants, to protect human living areas and their spheres of action, to build a firm system of inter-cooperation by supplying services to each other, it was necessary. But... He couldn't say that communication was an unequivocal success, as there were many obstacles.

One obstacle was the attitude of the robots. One of the orders hammered into the robots long ago was that they should be the ones to talk to the native inhabitants. When Kurobe talked to the true Sarulunia directly, they interfered. Even when he did talk, it was always with a robot-selected "educated colony". The robots believed it was totally unacceptable for him to converse with wild native inhabitants. Of course Kurobe, knowing the robots as well as he did, outwitted them several times and had spoken to wild native inhabitants, but each time he did the robots came running after him in a frenzy, and complained to him afterwards interminably. They believed that the "wild" ones were extremely dangerous.

The robots thought that way because of Kalgeist and his troops. To those who swore allegiance to the uniform, it was a standard conqueror's procedure to continue trying to injure those that maintained resistance, disguising their aggression as protection. Just as the Federation had used the same method elsewhere, so it was used here. In other words, some were called "educated", while the others were hunted by the soldiers. They tried to justify their position by claiming that since it was impossible to tell where young educated Sarulunia would emerge, they had to use force to prevent them from being eaten by the "wild" ones, and went so far as to enlist the aid of the robots and to control the landing zones of the flowers that danced up into the sky. The robots, programmed to believe human input, easily believed that the "wild" native inhabitants held some deep grudge against their human conquerors. He wondered how the true Sarulunia, faced with this, felt about humans, and he wasn't sure. To him – the Administrator trying to build a new inter-relationship of trust on this world – it was a major failure, an obstacle standing in his way.

The thing that bothered Kurobe the most was that communication itself was so difficult. Even with the translator device utilizing the highest human technology, and the help of the researchers, he could still only express the roughest of ideas. And, for exactly that reason, the researchers all too quickly adopted Kalgeist's bias, and came to look down on the native inhabitants. Still, the plan he was hoping to complete, even if he had the total support of the research community, was still a dream beyond a dream of mutual understanding.

Of course, he couldn't stop trying. He was in the position of having to prove the superiority of the Administrator system to them all. He had to embody the new system of planetary government, the new order that was absolutely impossible under military rule.

He was the Administrator.

He knew without having to repeat those facts again in his head, he already knew. He knew in his heart exactly what he must do.

But… Why was he so tired? What was this heaviness that was dragging him down? What was this forlornness that held him, like he was wandering through space?

The rain, as ever, continued to fall, yellow-green. The caravan of Kurobe and his robots proceeded ahead, colonies of true Sarulunia hidden in the rain to all sides. The flight of the flowers had just ended, so there were no flowers visible, and there were motiles standing in a line on the cleared ground. They were there to indicate respect for the Administrator. No mistake, the robots posted in this area had announced his visit in defiance of his command.

Silly – he chided himself. This was the most "educated" area, which was why the First Research Station had been established here; but he couldn't help but feel a sense of revulsion at seeing the slavishness of those motiles every time he came.

Where the colonies began to thin out, they came to the research station.

"Thank you for coming; it must have been a terrible trip. We've been waiting for you. In fact, we have something we'd like you to see. Come in, come in."

Station Chief Spencer, who had come out to meet him with his colleagues, greeted him ebulliently. Spencer had the same habit of putting his own research before everything else, as did all researchers who had put in years and years on strange worlds. They were all single, of course... Or at least, they had no legal mates under the laws of their home worlds. Despite his jovial exterior, deep in his heart he resented people who could cast even a little influence over his research. When it came time to justify his capacity and achievements, he was prepared to do almost anything – ever since Kurobe had noticed the real character of the white-haired Station Chief, he had cautioned himself not to respond too strongly to the other's jollity.

"Well, this ends the scheduled tour." After the usual whirlwind tour and some research reports, Spencer began talking animatedly. "As I mentioned before, I have an interesting scene I'd like you to see. I've made the preparations, if you'd care to go?"

"Go? Where to?"

"To Amilla Sector..." Spencer started to say, then corrected himself. "Excuse me, to be precise Sector 8-13. As you know, we've fallen into the habit of giving these areas the names of things we love... Amilla is the largest city of the world where I was born. Well, in any case, let's go to the north: it's only about two kilometers."

"And what will we see?"

"An arbitration," nodded Spencer. "There's a fight between two colonies, and we've been asked to arbitrate. I'm not totally unaware of modern governing policy... There've been similar things up until now, and we have to respond to their request. Anyway, I accepted, and I figured that since the Administrator hadn't seen such a thing yet, it'd be better to invite you along when you came today."

An arbitration.

Kurobe narrowed his eyes slightly. That was something outsiders shouldn't touch. Still, in response to a request from the native inhabitants, they couldn't help but go. Still... He felt a fierce anger at those true Sarulunia that had created this problem, which should have dealt with it themselves. He couldn't stand those who borrowed the hand of authority to solve problems they should have solved on their own.

Even so, it was a very attractive invitation to him – never having seen anything like it before. He decided to go with Spencer.

Spencer had ordered his own car to stand by, but sQ2 opposed that. sQ2 had judged that any car designed for the Station Chief's use couldn't guarantee the safety of the Administrator. Spencer yielded the car to sQ2's order, but insisted on riding with the Administrator, so as a result he and the Administrator rode with sQ2, while the other two researchers followed in the Station Chief's car. sQ7 came behind them, installed in a roving LQQY-type scout car. It was a strange lineup, but depending on the destination and the co-ordinates, the sphere of the robots' responsibilities overlapped, yielding this kind of half-baked job.

"Only two days ago, a representative of one of the colonies came to ask for assistance," said Spencer as the car began to move. "When I talked to them in the past, I told them to come by any time they had something to talk about. It was a real pain getting across the location of the research station, too. Still, the educated ones seem to understand somehow, and come every so often."

The rain had stopped. The cars, bouncing wildly, continued on.

"This is Amilla Sector."

It wasn't a very ordered place, and had thick woods. After asking Kurobe's permission, Spencer ordered the car to stop. "Well, let's get out."

Of course, sQ2 had a warning for them. "Be careful. This location is the border between educated and wild native inhabitants."

The two of them got down into the mud. The two other researchers, equipment in hand, were approaching quickly.

"It's over there," called one of them.

They left the line of cars, and walked forty or fifty meters through the trees and grass. sQ2, who couldn't move unsupported over the mud, was still warning something, but neither sQ7 nor one of the robot cars was dispatched to provide cover for him, perhaps because Kurobe and the others were wearing complete outside-use protective clothing.

The personnel in front stopped, and everyone else followed suit.

It was a very large colony, with a huge open space around it, and much vegetation, but the vegetation was spaced regularly every fifteen or sixteen meters.

There were three motiles moving around the colony, and, as if noticing the humans, many more came from the hemisphere, emerging headfirst. In all, about ten. The one advancing towards them was a slightly dark-colored motile, about one hundred eighty centimeters tall, its cluster of legs about as thick as a human arm, and its jelly-like vision organs looking every which way.

"That's the representative that came two days ago," whispered Spencer.

The motile stopped about a meter from the humans, and stood there hissing. They communicated by releasing water vapor through a hole in the top of their heads, controlling the expansion and contraction of the outlet.

By that time, one of the researchers had set down the translating device, and had finished adjusting it.

The device immediately began translating the motile's speech.

"Arrival happy. Under blessing of weather… Every day's water… The dawn that leads to flowers: true Sarulunia… Humans have come…"

From experience, it seemed that only the fixed phrases of greeting remained unclear, but still it seemed to be a very formal greeting.

"We troubled. We are educated xxxx [*meaning unclear*] number one clan… Very settled, big colony… We… Very close to us… Wild ones… Humans exterminate wild ones… Want humans to exterminate… xxxx is strong… Repayments are many."

"It seems to be saying about the same as what it said before," said Spencer, cutting the microphone. "They are enlightened, and very powerful. However, they can't expand because of the adjacent colony. If we exterminate it for them, they'll help us… And they said the adjacent colony is wild."

Kurobe nodded, but he didn't quite see the point. According to what he

28

had heard from Spencer, the usual battles of the true Sarulunia consisted of destroying each others' orchards and gardens, making the enemy motiles unable to ensure their own food supply, and forcing the others' home-tree to begin stretching towards other areas. Eventually, the original home tree would separate from the living areas, and rot, and the land would change hands. In more violent cases, the motiles would clash directly, ripping each other's skins, whipping their tendrils, kicking with their legs... In any case, the usual winner was the bigger, stronger colony.

But this... Wasn't this just the opposite?

"I wonder why?" Kurobe murmured unconsciously. "Why did they ask for our help?"

To Spencer, though, who had seen many similar things here, it was not such a major question.

"The bigger colony doesn't always win, you know. Maybe there aren't many cases of that happening, but there are at least a few examples. How about asking for yourself?" he said, handing over the microphone.

Kurobe took it automatically, and spoke after thinking a moment.

"Why did you request our judgment?"

When that had been translated and spoken by the translating device, the motiles stirred a little. There was an immediate answer.

The gist of it was that humans had conquered this world, so it was obvious that they should judge. It was their responsibility to abide by human decisions. They had been educated, so they knew the truth. They wanted to see how the humans would judge a fight between an educated colony and a wild one.

Kurobe grew tense. In that answer was a clear suggestion. The suggestion that humans should judge what was clearly in their own interest... This motile was much more cunning than he had expected.

Q: *Why don't you take care of it by yourselves?*

A: *It is for the conquerors to punish. It is not for us to punish those who disobey by ourselves. We must leave it to your judgment.*

Kurobe groaned. He was becoming progressively less and less happy.

They were trying to use humans. By following the rules closely, they were trying to take the prize. Spencer, who now felt like a real ruler, didn't notice.

He tried to call out the inhabitants of the adjacent, apparently deserted, colony. However much he called through the translator, though, there was no response.

He asked the motiles near him to bring out the others.

They refused. They said the other colony was wild, and therefore had no reason to respond.

"Well then, it's simple. We just judge them in absentia. In any case, since this side is communicating with us…"

Kurobe cut off what Spencer what trying to say.

"That's not possible. We must hear both sides."

Spencer fell silent, with a twisted smile on his lips.

Kurobe told the motiles to call out the others, by whatever means necessary. Without that, he said, this judgment may not go as you desire.

They reacted again, agitated. They looked like they wanted to say something, but at last moved off in a group.

They advanced on the smaller colony. Whipping their tendrils, trampling the vegetation, shredding the leaves…

They were attacking.

They were taking his words literally and beginning to attack. Having received permission to call out the enemy, they were using the chance to batter their way in.

I have to make them stop, thought Kurobe, when something came bounding out of the empty colony. In the blink of an eye, one, then two, of the attacking motiles were hit and fell.

It was – an inhabitant of the smaller colony. It moved so fast it almost didn't seem to be a true Sarulunia, but it was clearly a motile.

The group from the larger colony fell back awkwardly. When the other confirmed that they had returned to their own property, it turned, and made to re-enter the smaller colony.

"Wait," called Kurobe, agitated.

The motile stopped, and turned its vision organs his way.

Kurobe felt his breathing stop for a second or two. He had never felt a true Sarulunia to be beautiful before, but if it were possible for one of them to be beautiful, then the one standing in front of him was truly so. The skin was a faint pink, looking almost semi-transparent, and the vision organs were clear. It was a figure produced by a master sculptor... It was different from human ideals of beauty, but he had to admit it was stunning. Even though he had seen many motiles, he had never felt this way before.

Well, it was what it was. He fired off his question.

"I want to hear your side of this."

The pale pink motile said nothing in reply.

"We were requested to pass judgment by these motiles. They want us to remove you."

The other gave its first response. "You are not true Sarulunia."

"I am the Administrator. I am the person entrusted with governing this world. When requested, I must pass judgment."

"This is how all the wild ones are," interjected the representative from the larger colony.

"Do not interfere," said the pale-pink motile. "This is a problem of the true Sarulunia."

"But you should be able to let us hear your defense. We wish to solve this problem."

"You are human."

"Yes."

"Here is our place. We were here before. Humans came and hurt us. Our home-tree, eliminated. Our branch trees, eliminated, but for this single one. I am the only motile. Afterwards, xxxx clan came," the pink being said. "Human interference not needed. We will solve this with xxxx clan alone."

"..."

"xxxx clan is strong. And numerous. Our garden was destroyed. I collect food from the surrounding xxxx [*meaning unclear – untended*

31

areas?]. I will not surrender. I will not move, even if destroyed by xxxx clan. Do not interfere."

"…" Kurobe fell silent. He was moved. To Kurobe, who had seen many motiles trying to use human power, or trying to prove their slavishness, this was a fresh surprise. True, he had only met wild native inhabitants twice. Still, he hadn't thought they were very much different from the educated ones. Compared to them, this motile was…

Or maybe this was the standard for the wild ones. Maybe this was the true spirit of all the Sarulunia. Weren't all the true Sarulunia proud like this before being spoiled? As he thought that, he felt his anger towards those stationed here boil up.

And it might turn out all right, he said to himself. Maybe it would be possible to fulfill his command – to have humans and native inhabitants living together in true sympathy – by learning to understand the real spirit of these true Sarulunia they called "wild".

"Both sides have come out; it looks like you'll finally have to give some sort of a judgment," said Spencer, watching Kurobe's expression.

"Wait," said Kurobe. Before he himself knew it, he had assumed the position of this world's supreme authority, and it showed in his attitude. "There will be no judgment. It is cancelled."

"Cancelled? But… "

"There will be no such things as judgments from now on. We must strictly obey the established governmental policy. Native quarrels shall be handled by the native inhabitants – that is the heart of the Federation's Class III, Type B directive."

"What the hell…?" shouted Spencer. "Do you govern by whim? Is that what an Administrator is? Are you…"

He shut his mouth. Spencer knew that to go any further wouldn't help.

When he saw the Station Chief's reaction, Kurobe felt as if he had been dashed with cold water.

What are you doing? This isn't what you learned. Is this what an Administrator is? Isn't this just like being a dictator?

Reflecting, he softened his voice, and clapped Spencer on the shoulder.

"Well, let's do it this way. I'm only the representative of Federation policy... I can only do as they say."

Spencer didn't even try to smile. "I understand. Will you tell that to the natives there?"

Kurobe knew he had made a new enemy. He knew it, but there was nothing he could do about it right away. After some time passed, he would have to soften that enmity. Later.

Expressionless, he lifted the microphone, and made his pronouncement.

"There will be no judgment. There will be no more judgments from today. This will be formally announced later, but from now on all problems between true Sarulunia shall be decided by the true Sarulunia themselves."

The translator sounded, and the motiles from the big colony seemed stupefied. They probably wanted to complain, but couldn't find the courage.

The pale pink motile from the small colony stood there, rigid. It said nothing.

Watching it, Kurobe felt all the pent-up self-reproach come rising at once from his heart. What have we humans done to these native inhabitants? Though it wasn't he that had spoiled them, killed them, he must bear responsibility for it as a human... That was what he felt, and, unconsciously, he gave voice to his thoughts.

"We will not hunt your kind a second time. We will not discriminate between wild and educated. I promise this as an Administrator."

While that was being translated, he felt a warmth spread throughout his mind. It wasn't his own feeling. It was being sent from the outside.

What? What was it?

He lifted his eyes, and saw that the pale-pink motile had all its vision sensors pointed at him.

Was that...? Was it...?

Was it coming from that motile?

He stared at the other.

33

Again, the vision organs... But this time, a warmth with a bit of humor diffused throughout his being. It was an image of gratitude, and a smile.

Was this real?

Was that motile really sending it?

He felt the other confirm it. Without movement, or sound, or any expression, he knew the other's feeling. It was like the silent communication that two close friends use to understand each other without words.

"Well, let's go on back. What are you doing, just standing there?"

Urged by Spencer, he returned to himself.

Right.

The cross-flow he had felt just now had only been between the pale-pink motile and himself. Spencer and the others had felt nothing.

He couldn't believe it. The fact that the true Sarulunia should have that ability... No, not that. It was harder to believe that he himself had come to feel what he had. He hadn't felt this type of heart-to-heart communication for years. He could only remember it from long ago, before he underwent training as an Administrator — no, even before that, back in his childhood. Something he had forgotten, had lost, had given up as never to be returned to again: that was what he couldn't believe.

Was it then?

Was that when his inclination towards *something* had obtained real substance? Did he catch what he had been chasing, then?

Yes.

Watching the flowers flowing across the light-blue phosphorescent sky, he smiled a tired smile.

He couldn't deny it.

But... As a result, what had happened in his heart? Where was he running? Intending to be an Administrator, where had he become lost?

He knew.

He turned his face away from the window of the Administrator's Office. Now... Now that he was watching his eighth flight since he had been installed as Administrator... Those flowers were too gorgeous, too empty, too heavy on his heart. It still fascinated him, as it always did: that

34

was a fact. It was an addictive view that he couldn't run away from however much he tried.

Naturally, his impression of that stupendous view changed each time he saw it. The time he had just been assigned here... The second time... And then...

Didn't that in itself mean that he had come to change?

What had happened?

How was he decaying?

I know... he repeated the words again, deep inside.

Then, hadn't he once again grasped the hopes he had discarded years ago?

He believed that he had seen the real Sarulunia in that motile – the motile he had come to call Amilla, borrowing the name of the sector – and he thought to search out the character of the true Sarulunia through contact with that motile.

What he had come to remember, though, was not Amilla as a true Sarulunia, but the individual who was Amilla.

And as a result, he was shaking. Hadn't he come to doubt his worthiness for the title of Administrator?

He lifted his face again, and looked at the flowers filling the night sky. More than five minutes later, he pressed the "opaque" button, and left.

It was already time to sleep, but he didn't feel like activating the sleep device. He wanted to think some more.

He had found opportunities, and had gone to see that motile, Amilla. He explained to Spencer, and to SQ2, who always came along, that he wanted to see the outcome of the fight; but he really wanted to know the character of the true Sarulunia through Amilla, and search out the future paths for government.

No.

It wasn't that, really. Wasn't he really searching for that contact of two minds – by what means he didn't know – that communion? He was that uneasy, that hungry. He had gradually come to realize that, but his stubbornness kept insisting *No, it's not that, that's not your goal.*

That's why he never tried to tell Spencer about the experience of that flow. If he did, Spencer would try to repeat the experiment again, with no regard for Amilla at all. He couldn't stand that, and most of all he couldn't bear having the shame in his heart exposed.

That was when his infidelity to the post of Administrator really began. Amilla fought well against the xxxx clan's colony. It was hard to believe that a colony with only a single inhabitant could do so much, but it was a fact. Amilla covered its lack in numbers with unflagging effort and incredible speed, not allowing the neighboring larger colony's strategies to succeed. Not only that, but it even struck back, finally forcing them to withdraw from their home-tree. When that happened, Spencer's attention shifted to other events at other colonies, and Kurobe had to go to Amilla's colony alone. He quibbled with the robots, outwitted them, sometimes gave them direct orders, and managed to visit Amilla regularly.

He continued to see Amilla to fulfill his duty as Administrator. At any rate, that was the reason he started… He thought so, sitting on his bed.

When had he been forced to accept that it wasn't true any more? At the time of the fourth flight? The fifth flight? He couldn't say with con-

fidence. What he could say was that, even now, what he had been searching for was that flow of hearts. The feeling that he had experienced during that first flow just couldn't be duplicated. He found out much later
that it never occurred when Spencer was present. Subsequently, he only
felt a slight touch when he was exhausted from using the translator to
manage their tortuous communications, and he had to be content with
that for the day. It was a help that Amilla almost always came out when
he called, regardless of the time.

Still...

Since he had started going alone, the frequency of his visits had increased dramatically. No mater how poorly the translator worked, if he
received some emotion, then their mutual understanding became much
easier. If that became easier, then they could converse with even more
smoothness.

And so, like peeling back the layers of an onion, many things became
clearer to him.

He came to understand that the true Sarulunia were intelligent beings —
at least equal to humans, occasionally superior. That function awakened
and began to develop in the young ones that returned to their colonies
and became part of their home-trees. The home-tree itself had no intelligence, but seemed to act as a sort of data bank for the entire colony, and
the young ones were raised there, learning the basics until they could
safely become motiles. Once they became motiles, the home tree was no
longer a school, but more like a home, which provided a supply of water.

Amilla revealed that the motiles of a single colony could communicate
among themselves by telepathy. Their method of communicating by releasing water vapor, which had been thought to be their usual method of
conversation, was in fact analogous to human gesturing, and was used to
communicate with motiles from other colonies.

These kinds of facts, which humans were probably learning for the first
time, and which would probably make Spencer's eyes bulge if he heard
them, Kurobe disclosed to no-one. Since he had first felt that flow, and kept
it a secret, there had been no choice but to continue to hide it, keeping that

knowledge within himself. If he spoke, someone would sniff out his sense of solitude, of alienation, and it would result in a condemnation of all Administrators. If that happened, the special privilege he enjoyed in talking to Amilla would vanish as well.

He was talking about many things with Amilla, exchanging opinions about many concepts.

"You're not sleeping yet?" LQ4's contact suddenly interrupted.

"Not yet... A little longer."

"If you stay up too long, you will suffer from lack of sleep, and it will result in ill health. When do you intend to sleep?"

"Later. Won't you leave me alone, please?"

"Yes, sir. In that case, I will activate the sleep inducer in thirty minutes. Is that acceptable?"

"Mm."

What was he hungering for? Was it only the hope that something sweet would become his? He thought he wanted to extricate himself from this. At any rate, he believed that he had rid himself of these desires through his harsh training. Still... Human beings always had hopes at the bottom of their hearts, and those hopes would rise at the slightest opportunity, tormenting.

Well, that was how it was.

But why didn't Amilla feel the same?

"Even though I understand what you say, I can't feel the same way," said Amilla. "You have given many reasons for why you humans interfere with us, but I still can't comprehend it."

"I have come to protect this world, to return it as much as possible to its original state. I would like to build trust between our two races."

"If that's true, then why don't you just leave us alone? If nobody came, wouldn't that be enough? Your expansion of power is different from ours. We only fight to protect our source of life. If you don't need to do anything here, then there should be no need to conquer."

"..."

38

"And is mutual trust really possible? Between us it truly exists, but it happened by accident – because when I thanked you for your decision, I unwittingly used telepathy. If other motiles had been present at my colony, it would have been impossible. And you were in a state where you could receive it… That's why. Our relationship is not based on the exchange of material things, but is a spiritual one. Can this be fostered between groups of humans and groups of true Sarulunia?"

"It's different. That's…" but he couldn't complete it. By Amilla's way of thinking, it was just impossible to comprehend.

"You mentioned supplying human weaponry, but that's meaningless," said Amilla. "Why should I need weapons? To fight, we have legs and tendrils. It would be no victory to win by using something other than your own self. And to think of destroying entire colonies… The variety of the colonies can change from the genetic pattern of a single flower. If a colony vanishes, then doesn't that much potential vanish from the race?"

"Why do you flower?" he asked. "If you stay as motiles, you can have a long life as intelligent beings… Why do you throw that away, and become a wind-blown flower?"

"Desire," Amilla answered. "Your sleep? Or death? It's probably close to that. When you feel your usefulness to the colony has ended, then you choose to flower."

Amilla indicated its elders, which had returned to the home tree after many seasons as motiles, and begun to grow as soft flowers.

"These flowers are not really my colony. As the last of my colony, I had to let in young ones from other colonies. They end their cycles as motiles, fly as flowers, again return as young ones, and will be raised here as members of this colony. Until I see that happen, I have a purpose in living. If I lose my purpose…"

"You will flower?"

"Yes. I will rest."

"If you flower, your consciousness will vanish, correct?"

"The I of now will vanish."

"And you don't feel anything about vanishing?" asked Kurobe, trying to understand.

"Nothing," answered Amilla, with a satisfied expression.

At some point, LQ4 must have activated the sleep inducer. He noticed himself drifting off to sleep. *Amilla...* he thought. In another one or two seasons... Sometime, Amilla would flower. When that happened, he would lose the one he talked to.

Where would Amilla fly? Where would Amilla land? ...and what kind of spermatozoa larva would enter...? He bit his lip. He mustn't think about that disgusting, instinct-driven larva crawling into Amilla's flowered body. When he thought of that, he felt he would go crazy.

Jealousy? Maybe it was jealousy.

When had he begun to think of Amilla as a human woman?

Amilla was not a woman. Amilla was a plant.

He groaned, thinking of that plant.

Was what he was trying to do really possible? Was the government by mutual understanding that he and his fellow Administrators were trying to create really obtainable?

No. Could a real interrelationship grow between two different species? Could plants with different ways of thinking, different living environments, really grow together with humans?

Or... Kurobe suddenly thought: wasn't this Administrator system, this system that tried to create the ideal government by giving consideration to other races, wasn't it merely another decision made solely by humans? Wasn't such a thing impossible, thinking only of government? Or... Maybe Kalgeist and that patrol chief, and the others... Don't they all rule for many different reasons?

He grew too sleepy, and couldn't think anymore.

Tomorrow, I'll think.

Tomorrow would be a heavy day.

And the next day...

He slept. The flight of the flowers continued in his dreams, and Amilla was among those flowers. He was merely watching. He could never become a flower, and Amilla could never, ever, become a human being...

LQ4 turned out the lights – for the Administrator.

A Distant Noon

A DISTANT NOON

— I —

THE FLYER DROPPED, and then shifted back to level flight.

The sky ahead was purple. Across the purple heavens, the headlight beams shone golden, glittering, lighting up the countless raindrops like a mirage as the flyer pierced through the lavender darkness.

Mmm, it's started again.

Oki PPK Naska stared passively into the front glass for a while.

It's beautiful. So beautiful.

Why couldn't he always be like this, leaving his cares to the wind, relaxed? Before another minute passed, his field of vision became more colorful, changed faces to become a paradise of brilliant hues. Then, in an instant, it all concentrated to brilliant white, turned to flaming high noon. Why couldn't he immerse himself in that world, greedily devouring his dreams? That one last hope still surviving in his heart: wasn't that the only path back to peace, the peace he had only felt in childhood – or at least, that he thought he had felt?

Still.

Oki knew that the "mirage" was a psychological phenomenon caused in human beings by the repetition of twilight and night on this world, Nenegin. He also knew well that if the color-sense compensation effect was left untreated, it became much harder to restore normal vision. Once you entered the false noon of this world, you couldn't return to the real noon. Just like the colonists who had come here... No, the word "colonist" had a nice ring to it, but the fact was, they were social failures. They had become prisoners of this world, unable to escape it.

Oki forced out the pain and the almost-homesickness he felt in his heart, and, taking out the vision-restoring spray from his inner pocket, pressed it to his arm.

After a while, the drug took effect, and his color sense returned to normal. That normalcy, though, was of course only the usual blackness and silver spray of raindrops. Normalcy held no joy, no spaciousness: merely boredom.

Anyway... The color-sense compensation effect shouldn't occur again for another three or four hours. Considering his present condition, it should last that long. It was also a fact that the drug's effect grew weaker with each dose.

Mmm...

As long as you stayed here on this almost colorless Nenegin, the frequency of color-sense attacks grew higher and higher. If you wanted to avoid it, there were only two methods. One was to decorate your home in total color. The other was to stay awake as little as possible, increasing sleep time to the maximum. People who used the former method, though, became subject to extremely intense color-sense attacks later on, because their nervous systems, hungry for color, began to demand it aggressively after receiving it in small doses. Oki had discarded that method some time ago, as it was like giving a drink of seawater to a thirsty man, or a drug to an addict in withdrawal. From the latter approach, the only effect was that you didn't suffer attacks during sleep. And, in the waking that always followed sleep, there was always a washed-out feeling. The blank-mindedness of not knowing where you were, stopping the pendulum of your time sense, gradually led to a return to reality. And "reality" was the realization that you were adrift in a soggy hell.

There was no solution. As long as you were here on Nenegin, there was no help for it. There was no remedy other than to flee it. He, though, was in a position where that wasn't possible, wasn't permitted.

Of course, as far as appearances went, Oki couldn't hold that attitude. An Administrator should feel a sense of love for, a sense of difficulty in parting from, the world assigned to his care. And, because he was the Administrator, he mustn't feel hatred towards this world – or, more accurately, he was an Administrator, with the experience and training needed to become one with whatever world he might be entrusted with.

But he did hate this Nenegin. He hated everything on the surface of this world: the eternal rain... The succession of almost identical, lusterless days and nights under the thick clouds... The miserable, curious native inhabitants... And the humans who had come here to live, with their twisted society.

This place was different.

This world was fundamentally different from the other worlds he had served on, Yascalin and Todonin. At the start, they too had been strange places to him, but hadn't he managed to discharge the functions of an Administrator on those different worlds? Perhaps it was different from what he had considered ideal, but he had managed to comprehend it all in his own way. Here, though, he couldn't find such an opening, no matter how much time he spent. He himself couldn't yet figure out the reason why... He just didn't fit.

In spite of it (he thought to himself wryly) here he was on Nenegin. As the Administrator of Nenegin, as the hand of the Terran Federation, he had been fighting for over forty days to fulfill his orders. He was struggling under the load of this world's classification: Class III, Type C – the development of civilization. He was trying to answer the almost hopeless demand that the Federation thought was possible. No, not only that. Even if he did manage to fulfill this, somehow, there would be another demand afterwards – the demand to change to Type D: to help with the creation of a suitable environment for those who already had to live here, win their public support, and ensure their harmonious intercourse with the native inhabitants. Was that really possible? Was there really anybody who could do that?

The Federation had judged it to be possible, and for exactly that reason had dispatched the man who could do it. That man was the Administrator –Oki PPK Naska.

He questioned himself again.

Could he do it?

Did he really, honestly, intend to do it?

Answer... It didn't come. Or rather, from the start, there was only one answer. As long as he stayed within the Administrator system, the answer was settled. It was not acceptable to dodge things. Whether he succeeded or failed, the Federation would be the judge, and he had no choice but to continue until they made their decision. He could not judge things himself. Even if he were judged as having failed, and was transferred to a lower post with less difficulty, he would still be one of the elite. It was completely different from throwing away his duties, and falling into that "other" group.

Was that all?

Was that the only reason he was doing this?

Maybe.

At any rate, he couldn't say it wasn't with any certainty.

Oki, of course, never revealed the scorn he directed at himself. Administrators, who received such intensive training, never did. They were trained to control not only their expressions, but also what was in their hearts. Especially someone like him: a veteran of two other worlds. Those thoughts that came bubbling up from inside him were quickly compressed and locked up in a corner of his heart.

"In another twenty kilometers we will arrive at Pijajasta," reported SQ2A.

Oki strained his eyes, but he could see nothing more than before. Only blackness and rain.

"I will report the situation in Pijajasta as investigated in advance by LQQ72. Of the data now held, I will include only what is judged to be critical. Will you read the report? Or listen to it?"

"I'll listen."

"Understood... The community called Pijajasta consists of approximately seven thousand native inhabitants. As determined by the preliminary investigation, it is the largest community known to the Administrator's Office. On the Yorkland measurement scale, the natives' average intelligence level is 3.41; the upper one percent is 4.40. However, their performance as a group is nine percent compared to the theoretical maximum, which places them very high for their relative living standard, although they are still at the pre-organized society level."

"..."

Oki listened silently. It wasn't a good idea to ask questions when a high-level robot was talking. They were talking based on their own logic systems, and to interject a question often derailed their train of thought. After pursuing the tangent suggested by the question to the bitter end, and explaining every detail, they would then return to the main topic. They tied everything together, never missing a point. In order to return to the main topic, it might take hours of explanation. Of course, an order to stop could be given, but you had to be prepared to listen to it later, because the robot would explain it. Although it could be thought of as a fault, the current Administrator system was based on robots, and this situation had been born of necessity. Without their functions, the Administrator's job would be extremely difficult. Since all the Administrators knew the characteristics of the robots thoroughly, there was no need to change. As long as the robots fulfilled their assigned functions, no one cared to do anything else. In general, bureaucracy was like an involuntary muscle, and rather than using it badly, it was safer to maintain control by stimulating it, damping it, stopping it. You could say that handling the robots followed along the same lines.

"LQQ72 has announced our visit to the political body of Pijajasta," continued SQ2A. "It reports that the native inhabitants are making preparations to greet us."

" … "

"The report is concluded. Do you have any instructions or directives?"

At that point, Oki spoke.

"I want to verify something… Has it been made clear that we have come in response to their request?"

"Yes, as per your directive received before we left."

"Satisfactory." Of course the robots weren't likely to forget to do something. Rather, he had asked the question to firmly pound it into his own head.

"We will land in a few minutes. I will inform you when we land," reported SQ2A, and then fell silent.

Oki felt the light humor of the situation.

In a few minutes…

Really, robots that learned to use that kind of imprecise, everyday speech – especially high-level robots – seemed to want to use it at every opportunity.

That was not his deep feeling, but rather a passing fancy. To the Administrator, robots were just perfectly constructed tools.

On the other hand, he also knew well that they were tools of unmistakable authority, and possessed the highest capabilities for the oppression of lower levels. Any Administrator, looking back on himself and his own authority, would soften his position, because any criticism would pass over the robots, exactly because they were not human, and concentrate on him. Of course, he would only soften a little, a slight mental relaxation. That, though, would never become an excuse for him. He always said to himself that, even from the political viewpoint, they had no effect on the Administrator, and it was meaningless to debate the point.

Oki cut off his thoughts there. He realized that he had become too tense as the craft descended.

They landed at Pijajasta.

When he took one step outside in his protective clothing, the world was nothing but mud and rain. The green-brown mud vomited bubbles of gas incessantly, and the rain continued to pour down from above. Without testing each place, it was impossible to guess the depth of the mud. If it went as far as ten centimeters, there were places where it went as deep as several meters. That was what it was like on the surface of Nenegin. There were active volcanoes across the planet, and, as one could imagine, it was hot, and the mud itself swarmed with life of all kinds.

Oki, together with SQ2A, advanced across the mud wearing float shoes. To use float shoes required a great deal of training and concentration. It was much easier to use a boat... But after considering the damage to his authority as an Administrator that would follow if his boat should overturn, he decided it was better to use the float shoes, however cumbersome they were.

Encircling him and SQ2A were the protective LQ-class robots, each a cubic meter or so in size. Each one was like a fully automatic heavy tank, but with decision-making capability and fighting power not found in tanks. Administrator Oki could place all his confidence in their capabilities. Just as the old monstrous surface ships that crossed the Pacific scared away the sea life with their shapes and engine noise, making it impossible to come truly close to the sea, so did these robots make it difficult for the Administrator to approach the native inhabitants and hold true communication. In time – or rather, as soon as possible – he wanted to be able to meet with the native inhabitants without robot protection, but at the moment he lacked the confidence. He just had to be patient until it became possible. Until then, he had to stay inside their protective shelter. His protection, he thought, included a heavy minus as well. Well, maybe that was good. But in his heart, Oki wondered if the day would ever come when he could walk freely without protection.

With the long-frequency visor added to his protective clothing, his field of vision became bright. It raised the infrared wavelengths to where they became visible. To meet the native inhabitants he had to use it, no matter how much he disliked it. It wasn't night now, which helped quite a bit, and he could make out shapes even with the naked eye. Naturally, a normal light was out of the question. To these dwellers-in-the-darkness, a normal light caused sunburn, headaches, and in extreme cases even blindness – a harmful, too-bright-to-be-visible brilliance. If the visor were only more complete, as Oki desired, he would use it constantly. In other words, if the colors and everything else returned to normal along with the frequency shift... Even though his vision became brighter, it was still a picture drawn only in rust, red, deep crimson, cinnabar, and black. He just couldn't come to like the strange, illusory feeling caused when all colors were compressed into the red and orange shades.

Around the party, dozens of native inhabitants thrust their heads up out of the mud, and swam around. Occasionally, a raft made of branches with two or three crew on board would drift near, but upon seeing Oki and his robots, they hurriedly changed course.

Native inhabitants.

To be precise, the "Nenegia" – the dominant species on this world, Nenegin.

Every time Oki saw one of them, he felt a sense of disbelief. There was no mistake that they were at the top of the ladder on Nenegin. Although it was pretty crude, they had their own distinct civilization... But he still couldn't believe it. The reason, more than likely, was because of their appearance.

Their average height was about one hundred fifty centimeters, and all of it looked funny. Protruding pig eyes, a mouth stretched sideways... Their ears, breathing holes, and gills were lined up on the sides of their heads, leaving a blank space in their faces where humans had a nose. The vestige of a vertebral fin rose on the back of their heads. All together, the head and face were huge compared to the body, plus which they had egg-shaped protruding bellies and water-flippers for feet. Their legs were strong enough not only to propel them through the mud, but also to kick enemies to death if need be. Their legs had evolved to the point where they could stand erect, and as a result their upper limbs had changed to supple arms, with four nimble digits.

Now that he thought of it, they looked like puffed-up frogs or swimming pigs. It was only reasonable that he should have trouble believing that things with their appearance could be intelligent. He had studied about them and their manner of living before coming here, and he learned more from the robots, and from direct communication, but he still had the same strange feeling as before. To the colonists who had come here and built their own little closed world, the Nenegia were merely objects of scorn. The Terran Federation forbid the colonists to take that attitude, but the Federation was very far away and the edict was not very strong, so it was generally not expected to be obeyed. With an Administrator present, they at least shouldn't try to enslave or kill the native inhabitants. He had the authority to order them to stop, and to send robot watchers into the colonists' living areas. If they resisted that action, it was not hard to imagine what his political reaction would be. Oki knew how they felt about the Nenegia – the pig-frogs. And the fact was, he had to admit deep in his heart that the name was perfect, absolutely perfect.

The party was already approaching the gate, which was flanked on either side by watchtowers. They were not just heaped-up mud, of course, but cleverly assembled piles of branches and roots, with openings where the gatekeepers would watch the traffic. It afforded protection not only above the surface of the mud, but also in the mud itself: there was usually a strong movable wall under the surface. It was to guard against entry by the giant, multi-fanged predatory fish, and the fierce soft-bodied creatures, but at the same time it was also used for defense against other Nenegia, when there was a war for some fishing ground or feeding matter. This gate and its equipment were superb, in keeping with this largest known settlement, Pijajasta.

At the moment, it was completely open. There was nothing at all in the waterway to impede the progress of this special guest.

After they passed through the main gate, they entered the central waterway, and proceeded straight down it.

On both sides of the main waterway were further fences. On the far sides of those fences was more mud, then more fences, and so on and so on. From what they currently knew about the Nenegia, this was a collection of homes, ranging in size from four or five square meters for a small dwelling up to two or three thousand square meters for a mansion. Each was surrounded by a fence, which prevented entry either over the mud or through it, except through a gate. Each cluster of Nenegia homes had a fort that reflected its power, which was occupied by the leader of the group. As an independent communal group expanded through reproduction and adoption, it also produced buffer groups to help protect it from threats from the outside, leading to the development of towns. After the size of the community passed a certain point, food supplies came to be held in common, and the communal group began managing resources for the community, requiring a central government. In general, this took the form of the member second to the leader attending to the functions of government in the leader's name, and for the leader's benefit, but there were many different styles and levels of use for governments depending on the area. However, the bigger the community was, the more complicated and multi-functional became its government. As management became more difficult, more and more individual groups lost their defining characteristics. In that kind of society, where ability counted for more than lineage, and where there was a class of government officials without ties to a particular home, power had the tendency to shift from the separate homes to the central authority.

Oki didn't study all of this as recorded history. The Nenegia didn't really have anything yet that could be called "history", except for some oral traditions. All across Nenegin, the Nenegia were at about the same level of development, which one could easily understand with reference to the laws of history by which humanity had advanced. They were just now moving from towns to primitive city-states... No, it would be better to say from a feudal society to a stage preparatory to an industrial revolution. Oki had reason to think that. Here, among themselves, in this community, they had currency. They had been seen using the eyeballs of their most prized fish as exchange tokens.

All of the things he had seen so far had led him to believe they were at that level. Of course, he and the robots had no idea how things would change from here, or whether or not they would ever develop a true community consciousness. It looked as though they would not fall into a cycle of continuous stealing from each other, of conquering and being conquered. It was the duty of the Administrator to predict the future of the Nenegia, and both he and the previous Administrator had struggled with no avail to understand it.

To find out the answers, the only shortcut was to find the most advanced, or the largest-scale, community. The previous Administrators had all tried to investigate this largest community, Pijajasta, but with no success. The reason was that, for their own defense, the Nenegia had a custom of never revealing the interior features of their communities to any outsider. Oki, too, had tried to investigate the town, but had met the same barrier – and, until today, he had not been able to enter Pijajasta.

True, the robots had investigated under his instructions. They had managed to learn many things, such as the name – "Pijajasta". According to the native inhabitants, that was not really correct, but humans couldn't duplicate their pronunciation. Still, it was a proper noun, and it couldn't be helped. The robots cleaned up the pronunciation for humans, and that's how the name had been used ever since.

That level of investigation by itself, though, was not enough. However much data there was, the Federation wanted the judgment of the Administrator himself on the most critical things, which meant that he and his party had to go themselves.

They had sought the opinions of the colonists who had come to live on Nenegia. The previous Administrator had done that... Since Oki had had a bad experience when he first came here, he had lost trust in the colonists, and the more he found out about them, the less he liked them. Now he only maintained the minimum level of contact with them. In any case, they were not true colonists, and weren't recognized or protected by the Federation. The Administrator would face no difficulty in simply ignoring them, and he certainly didn't feel like asking anything of them.

Besides, he had managed to enter Pijajasta without their help. He could investigate, see this Pijajasta with his own eyes, without using the capabilities of the robots from the side or from the air. Of course, that wasn't to say he or other Administrators had never entered a community. They had entered small one near the Administration Complex often, and good-sized communities several times... But this was a giant community, quite possibly at a different level of development.

The fact that he had been so lucky was actually almost a mere coincidence. LQQ72, who patrolled this community regularly, had received a petition to meet the Administrator. Not only that, but it asked for the Administrator to meet them here, in Pijajasta. It was a longed-for, almost impossible-to-believe invitation that they had never made before.

The rain was falling, everything was red, and the float shoes were heavy.

Ahead of them was a hill-like structure. As they approached it, surrounded by the mud, it looked more and more forbidding.

The central fort.

Just as each member group had a fort to show its own strength, so did Pijajasta itself have a fort, and it was natural for it to be the seat of government... He had never seen such a large central fort.

It wasn't the standard uniform shape, but rose in a complex terraced formation, with fields on the terraces.

On the lower part, thirty or forty Nenegia were lined up, looking like a reception committee.

LQQ72 rose up out of the group of Nenegia, and came flying towards him through his red field of vision.

Oki couldn't detect it, but in that instant, advance scout LQQ72, SQ2A in charge of his protection detail, and the head SQ1, back at the main complex, were exchanging information, calculating and deciding. The fact that they made no effort to stop him meant that they felt there was no danger at the moment.

As LQQ72 joined them, the reception party began to move also, and a raft with four or five Nenegia on it came from the main fort. As they came, they croaked a subdued "*Ueyy, Ueyy.*"

"Welcome. We have been waiting. Please step up onto the raft," spoke the translator built into SQ2A's body.

Oki stepped onto the raft, still wearing his float shoes. SQ2A immediately took up a position at his side, and the other robots surrounded the raft.

The raft was big enough that there was still ample space even after Oki's party got on.

After he got on, the Nenegia said nothing, merely standing rigidly in respect. They seemed to be only underlings assigned to come meet him. To indicate their status, the Nenegia sewed a piece of rope or wood, called a *peda* (sometimes *peta*), on to the top of their heads, which bobbed incessantly. The material used to make them changed constantly from place to place, but the thinner it was – and the more there were – indicated higher status. The *peda* of Pijajasta were extremely thin, and wrapped in something soft, showing that a great deal of labor had been invested in making them, but the Nenegia here only had one or two *peda* apiece.

Oki turned to look at the stern of the raft, surprised. Generally Nenegian rafts, especially big ones like this, were propelled by a number of paddlers from the lower classes, kicking with their feet. This one, however, had some *peda*-less Nenegia turning a circular contraption, which transmitted its power to the mud and propelled the craft – a mud-wheel.

Oki was given no time to look at it, though. The raft arrived at the main fort, and all of the waiting Nenegia fell to all fours and croaked "*Guwa, Guwaa*" at him.

"Welcome to Pijajasta!" honked the translator. "Please step up onto the fort."

Oki began to climb the reddish-black rain-sprayed central fort. He noticed for the first time that it had real stairs built in.

And more… Oki felt his curiosity bubbling up even more. What had looked like terraced fields were divided into various levels, each with a number of Nenegia working on something or having some kind of discussion. As he climbed up the fort, he noticed that there were only one- and two-*peda* Nenegia visible. Generally, the standard group wore five or six, and the highest decision-maker a dozen or more.

He finally reached the top of the rain-drenched fort.

A single Nenegia popped out of the fort from one of the countless openings, padded around to the front of Oki, and signaled the others to fall back. Prostrating himself in front of Oki, he began to speak.

The translator spoke in turn:

"We have been waiting for you. I am… [*the translator paused, and converted it into human pronunciation*] Gugenge. I am the first decision-maker of Pijajasta."

"…"Oki had been expecting a long, drawn-out affair of ceremonious phrases when meeting the highest Nenegia, and was taken by surprise.

Was this really the first decision-maker?

His brick-red shiny skin and bulging eyes were certainly standard for Nenegia, maybe too standard, and the upper classes were usually a little fat. Also, this Nenegia had only a three-rod *peda* attached to his head.

Was this really the first decision-maker? Or merely a stand-in?

In any case, since the other had spoken, he had no choice but to return the greeting.

"I am honored by your invitation," he said, giving a small bow. "We were told you wished to meet with us. What is your desire? We would like to help you as much as we may."

"When you speak that way, it is so much easier to discuss things," said the Nenegia named Gugenge, standing up slowly. "We have something we would like to ask of you as Administrator."

"…"

"It is truly a selfish request, though…"

"… I wonder what it might be?"

"Would you be willing to lend us one of your machines?"

"Machines?" Oki furrowed his brow. "We have many machines. What type of machine are you interested in?"

"Your laser."

"Laser?"

"Yes. The thing that produces invisible energy that destroys what it contacts."

"I would like to inquire," said Oki, on the alert, "Exactly how did you learn the word laser?"

"We heard it from humans."

"Humans?"

"Yes. Humans who live apart from you and your robots. We sometimes go there and trade our products for what they have. I saw it once, and was taught the word."

"I see," nodded Oki. He was talking about the colonists. Oki knew that there was barter between them and the Nenegia.

"But in that case, why don't you borrow it from them?"

"Because they won't loan us one," answered Gugenge. "They said, though, that you do not attempt to live with them… And, they complain that you are too friendly with us. So, I thought if I asked you, you might assist us in the matter."

"Depending on the use, that is a very dangerous device. How do you plan to use it? Not for war, surely…"

"War?"

"Don't you often fight among yourselves, your communities?"

When he heard that, Gugenge gave what looked like a strange smile.

"If we used the laser in fighting, we would destroy our prize. War is to capture talented Nenegia, and take the best fish. Is there any use for dead Nenegia? Can our warriors alone carry the captured fish? Pijajasta is the largest community. Not only the largest, but also possessed of a large force of talented members, and we are raising more. Our fish are more abundant that anywhere else. Why should we have to fight?"

"Don't they ever come attacking you?"

"We have managed to protect Pijajasta until now. Even if we don't have your laser, we can continue to protect it, I'm sure. If we have the laser, then they certainly won't come invading. All in all, there is no possibility of the laser being used in combat."

"..." Oki stared silently at the other. This Nenegia was different from the others. He thinks a lot better than any other I've met, he said to himself.

"We wish to use the laser for development," continued Gugenge. "We are undertaking many projects to make Pijajasta a better place for us to live in. For that purpose, though, we must cut and work not soft materials, but hard materials. What now takes many members a long time to perform could be done quickly with your laser. That is why we have asked you..."

"I see." Oki gave no answer.

Maybe it was a lie. Maybe they planned to use it in war. Still, if that became a problem, then he could simply take it back. That, along with punishing the government of Pijajasta, would settle the problem. If he simply warned them in advance, there should be no problem.

And if the laser could be genuinely useful to the Nenegia... They could begin to develop a proper civilization...

That was it.

He had been changed by the Federation with this world as Class III, Type C – the development of civilization.

For that reason, wouldn't it be better to respond positively to their request? He should, even if there were problems, go along with what the government of Pijajasta was attempting to do, cooperating with and guarding them.

"If you loan us a laser, then we will be able to believe in your kind." Maybe Gugenge thought Oki's silence was hesitation, and cast out more bait. "In that case, although it's an exception to our rule, we would be willing to guide you through Pijajasta."

"What!?" At those words, Oki lost the train of thought he had already decided on.

The chance!

No human had ever seen the interior of Pijajasta closely. Not only would the Federation gain precious data, but there was no mistake that Oki's credit would rise, too. Plus which, it was close to what the Federation had ordered him to do here.

"If that is insufficient, then we are willing to pay compensation," continued Gugenge.

"Compensation?" asked Oki, his curiosity aroused in spite of his decision. "In what, your local currency?"

"No," contradicted Gugenge. "We could not pay you enough in our fish-eyeball currency. We would have to give you our high-denomination currency."

"High-denomination? You have such a thing?"

"Yes. Shall I show it to you?"

Gugenge bellowed something, and a single Nenegia dove into an opening for an instant, and brought out something in its hand, which it gave to Gugenge. He held it out in the palm of his moist hand.

"This single piece has the value of three thousand of our usual currency. Would it be acceptable to you if we paid one of these every day?"

"..."

Oki silently looked at the "high-value" currency in the other's hand.

What the...?

It was an ultra-durable, plastic – clothes button!

He couldn't imagine what road it had traveled over to reach Pijajasta, but it was clear where it had come from.

The colonists' area.

For Nenegian goods, the colonists handed these over in return. The Nenegia only saw humans dressed in protective clothing, which had no buttons. And so the colonists had given them buttons, which could be produced in any quantity by an automatic machine. The colonists here were doing exactly what other colonists had once done to Native Americans, with glass beads and knives.

Swindling them.

Of course, Oki didn't say that to the other.

He would have to settle things with the colonists later, he thought, as he replied to Gugenge.

"There is no need to spend these. You have said you will not use the laser for warfare. In the event you should violate that promise, not only will we take direct action to end its use by Pijajasta, but we will also judge each individual decision-maker here. Those are the conditions for loaning the laser."

Those words were immediately translated into Nenegian. The words themselves should have already been translated by SQ2A to SQI in the Administration Complex, and recorded there. He couldn't say what opinions or judgments SQI might have, but it certainly couldn't argue with a decision made based on his authority as Administrator.

"Thank you for your precious gift," responded Gugenge. "And thank you for allowing us to keep our high-denomination currency. Though Pijajasta is richer than all other communities, and has many more of them, they are still valuable…"

Gugenge prostrated himself again, then stood and signaled something to the waiting Nenegia, and approached.

"Since you have decided, I would like to guide you through Pijajasta."

In the red twilight, the ever-present rain was still falling, making everything appear black. That liquid blackness sprayed from his feet, spread out to pools of blackness, ran away, down, down. Gugenge and the other Nenegia were all red. Even SQ2A was just another member of the reddish-orange world.

This was a nightmare… Not reality, but an illusory vision that might possess him at any time… Oppressed yet again by that feeling, he tried to dispel it as he walked with the others down the central fort.

Midway down, Gugenge stopped and turned, indicating a single opening.

"We Nenegia live in the interior. Will you see it?"

"Yes, I'd like to," answered Oki immediately, climbing down a ladder after Gugenge.

It was dark, and it got darker as he went down.

Even with the vision aids, he couldn't make it out clearly. Still, through his squinted eyes he could make out a number of tunnels fanning out and down from his position, with some sort of bags hanging from the ceiling, and a number of Nenegia working here and there.

Below that was mud. A mud surface where a number of Nenegia were rising and submerging.

"What is under the mud?" asked Oki, feeling the overpoweringly heavy reverberations of his own voice.

"It's the same in the mud," replied Gugenge. "When we Nenegia emerge from the mud, we can use our vision, but we use our hearing in the mud. Not only that, but we can use our skin also to a certain extent... And we know what is happening, who is there. Of course, we have to make out detailed work with our fingers."

Oki didn't ask any more questions. The fact that these advanced, differentiated amphibians led such lives had already been hypothesized and verified. Still, when it was explained to him so simply, it all seemed to be blatantly obvious.

He decided to examine sq2a's recorded memories later, and climbed back up. Emerging, he went down the fort again.

A raft similar to the previous one was waiting on the mud surface. Two Nenegia were seated to the sides of that wheel-like arrangement, as before. Oki couldn't determine if it was the same one as before or not.

The raft started when Oki, Gugenge, sq2a, and three or four other Nenegia got on.

The lq-class robots surrounded the raft at a distance, and moved forward with it.

"We invented this propulsion device ourselves. It is vastly more efficient than the previous methods," said Gugenge.

"You did?"

"Yes. Not only this, we have designed and built many tools ourselves."

"..." Oki looked at the other in surprise.

"We have ten [*the translator stopped for a minute, then found a translation*] researchers here," he continued. "Two of my brothers work as researchers, and there are some who used to be in the lowest class. Class distinctions are not important. We will give special treatment to any member with ability... Each of these researchers has a number of assistants, and works on developing new tools. This system works very well, and we are thinking of developing it into something bigger."

"..."

"Our inventions will gradually gain acceptance in other communities and be used there. And Pijajasta will become even more prosperous."

"... I see," murmured Oki.

"I have thought about why other communities do not feel as we do. The answer is clear. The other communities are too finely segregated. The first-level decision makers, the high-, medium- and low-level decision makers, major group heads, medium group heads: they are divided without end; and, what's more, the occupation of each is defined by his social position. This makes it impossible to bring out the capabilities of the lowest classes and the slaves, even if they have true ability. Isn't that correct?"

"Just as you say." Oki began to feel queerly overpowered. "The social distinctions are not that strong in Pijajasta?"

"We want it that way, but it just isn't feasible. We have eliminated slavery. It's not efficient... The ones moving the raft now are free Nenegia. They get paid a reward, to the extent that there are too many applicants for the positions. I feel this is a good thing, but how do you feel?"

"What you say about slaves is correct... But if you only give special treatment to those employed by the government, when you finally exceed the limits of your managerial ability..." Oki remembered that the other was a Nenegia, and stopped. He had been feeling as if he were talking to an Administrator trainee. "Ah... Isn't it perfectly reasonable for the present?"

"Oh. We will think it over again carefully," answered Gugenge, and put his hand to his head. "Honestly, I would like to dispense with these."

"What? Oh, the *peda*?"

"Yes. Without them, the various members of Pijajasta could talk together much more easily. Our *peda*, though, are top quality, and sell for a high price, and we must display them to the other communities to sell them. That's why we wear them. Plus which, there are only a few people, even here in Pijajasta, who agree with me. Most of them still want the *peda*... To reduce their number, I explained that one of our *peda* has the value of three of any other make; I had to convince them of that. I think it would be better to stop pushing there, don't you?"

"Without investing a great deal of time, you will never succeed in that kind of change."

As he answered, Oki suddenly realized that Gugenge was – a reformer! He was advancing reforms actively, with his better-than-average clear thinking and sensitivity. The fact that this decision-maker had asked to meet with Oki had two important goals. True, he wanted to borrow the laser, but not that alone. Gugenge knew that the Administrator was a professional decision-maker, a specialist in government, and was aiming to utilize that specialized knowledge. He, who had only the talents he was born with as a reformer, realized his own weaknesses, and was trying to cover them with more advanced techniques learned from the Administrator. Why else would he guide him so politely, explaining everything, except to try to gain the friendship of the Administrator?

Oki had to admit that Gugenge was a rare genius among the Nenegia.

The raft turned right at a major intersection of waterways, skirted a patch of fecund vegetation that had risen up above the surface, and continued. That growth was shining, and would shine in one area while dulling in another, exactly as if it were breathing. That was a common feature of vegetation on Nenegin, where infrared rays were changed into short-wave radiation by a type of fluorescent effect.

But Oki hadn't known it could rise up like this, mounded.

"Our food areas are surrounded by that type of forest," said Gugenge. "You can't see it, but when you protect your food with a poisonous barrier like that, no one approaches. If the guards close the gate, that's enough."

In front of them, a wide water gate appeared...

The room seemed a little warm, so Oki turned down the heat and continued working. "Fifteen minutes until departure," came SQ2B's voice through the contact. After that announcement, though, SQ2B said nothing.

If it was only fifteen minutes until departure, SQ2B should have been urging him much more strongly by now.

Departure.

He had to put in an appearance at the meeting the colonists called a party. Oki would have preferred to avoid going if possible. But with their incessant invitations – and the indication from the robots that it had become a custom for the current Administrator to show up at their once-a-year parties – he had decided to go.

Once a year.

Of course, that followed the custom of once every three hundred sixty-five days. On this world, a day was twenty-six Terran hours long, but the Nenegia divided it into eight *shaga* (depending on the region, sometimes *shuuga*), and divided each *shaga* into sixty-four *chuga*. In addition, a year here was actually a little less than four hundred fifty days... The colonists had adopted the twenty-six hour day, but stubbornly refused to accept any of the others, holding to their Terran counterparts.

Oki had never been to a colonial party before. After he had considered the ridiculous event that had happened when he was first installed here, he thought he could imagine it pretty well.

The day he had taken office, the colonists had greeted him with wild cheering. Lighting for normal humans was too bright for them, as they had adapted to this world's strange visual effects, so they were all wearing dark glasses. Those men and women, wearing dark sunglasses and exotic clothing, shouted, pulled him into their midst singing, forced an alcoholic drink into his hand, and tried to crown him king. They said it was a crown symbolizing the ruler of the Nenegia. Oki had grown angry, and had driven them out of the Administration Complex. That unpleasant memory still clung to the inside of his brain, even now.

After he had lived there for a while, the robots told him that even though the previous Administrators hadn't liked it either, they sometimes met with the colonists, and allowed themselves to be crowned in some sort of ritual. sq1, the chief of all the robots on this world, had suggested to him that it might be best to do the same, but Oki had never agreed. Those who were called "colonists" here were merely travelers from another world, or those who had stopped off here for a time, and they were not officially recognized by the Federation. It was sufficient for the Administrator to do only the bare minimum for them – or so he believed. If they had time enough for this kind of thing, then they should be mingling with the native inhabitants, lending their hands to help them raise their civilization. If they who called themselves colonists cooperated with his orders it would be different, but they wanted to make trouble instead. They could go do whatever they wanted to. They should thank him for not simply driving them off the surface of the planet.

That there was a difference between his thinking and the thinking of the previous Administrators, all of whom had received proper training, showed that there were personality differences between Administrators. And age differences. Over thirty years had passed since the Administrator system had started. Over that period, the outside power blocs had changed, and as a result the Administrators and their training had changed as well. Of course, the fact that the older Administrators should change their thinking as a result of experience was only natural, too. All of the previous Administrators here on Nenegia had been older people. Compared to them, Oki was a younger Administrator than most, but also one who had scored an impressive list of achievements.

Well, it didn't really matter. Oki had said he would attend their party, and an Administrator wasn't allowed to break his promise.

He had been right in the middle of things, but he had to break it off.

He thought he would continue again after he returned.

Recently, Oki was burning with energy for his work. He had received work he could get lost in again, and his despondency was buried.

He was preparing to submit his investigation of Pijajasta, with an analysis, to the Federation. Since his first visit, he had returned to Pija-jasta three times, and his interest mounted each time.

Of course, Gugenge and his fellow officials guided him. Gugenge explained the situation and his future plans eagerly, and sought Oki's opinion constantly. Oki became convinced that Gugenge was hoping to use knowledge and techniques gained from him in these conversations – conversations with the Administrator, from another world.

He had been shown the interior of Pijajasta many times, and had investigated the translator's (SQ2A's) observation records afterwards, learning countless previously unclear facts about the living conditions of the Nenegia.

It was already known that the Nenegia lived in the mud, but it had not been known before that the fort was made up of numerous rooms and storehouses. Furthermore, none of it was privately owned, but rather belonged to the "house" – managed by the group leader – or, in this case, the decision-makers. Their tactile sense was developed as much as their vision or hearing, so that even in the mud they could distinguish each other and communicate merely with their fingers and skin… And many other facts became clear, too…

And also…

When he heard what these Nenegia were trying to add to the traditional life of Pijajasta, Oki felt the first continuing excitement since he had come to this world.

The reformers of Pijajasta had already begun to use letters. Previously, the Nenegia had used carved objects for signals, and huge bas-relief carvings in mass rallies, but Gugenge and his group were trying to advance that to the point of a symbolic writing. Because it had to be legible even in the mud, it consisted of a set of coded holes in a board. According to Gugenge, the one that had invented and perfected it was Gugenge's father, who had been a group leader of a large family group, and who had tried to spread it throughout Pijajasta with the help of his wife, who had come from the family of the first decision-maker. Gugenge also planned to carry it to the point where it was fully usable.

His group had also expanded the manufacturing groups, making factories on a huge scale. These factories consisted of dozens of Nenegia on the levels inside or outside the main fort, nimbly finishing off one piece at a time. Gugenge revealed that he had finally managed to make a production line process.

They were trying to accomplish so many things, too numerous to mention. Starting with loosening the caste system, they were also pushing hard at breaking down the strict linear ownership of goods within a single group, accelerating the invention of new tools and goods, and improving management techniques for their farms.

As promised, Oki lent them a laser device, which they soon mastered and began to use on new tools, as Gugenge had said they would.

The more he learned of the Nenegian way of life, the more Oki was impressed by the abilities of Gugenge and his group. There was no mistaking that they were a new generation of reformers, following in the footsteps of Gugenge's father, but they were pursuing their vision much more powerfully and with a higher consciousness than the previous generation.

Of late, Oki had come to think that maybe Gugenge's group and the previous group, too, were both spontaneous mutations. Spontaneous mutations usually appeared in groups after a while, and perhaps that accounted for Gugenge and his followers. And their group was fulfilling a role in thrusting their society ahead, raising the standard of living by leaps and bounds. Oki felt that he was lucky just to be on the spot when it happened.

Still, after a number of visits to Pijajasta, he noticed that what Gugenge was doing did not receive the total support of all the inhabitants. There were still many who held to the traditional beliefs, especially the group leaders, who should have been included in the ruling class. Although the amalgamation of the various houses was well advanced, there were still a number of large, powerful houses that remained independent. Their leaders criticized the sudden reformations, continuously opposed them, and took advantage of every opportunity to try to return Pijajasta to its traditional form. The fact that everything was working now was because

Gugenge's policies had made Pijajasta prosperous, and brought in profit for the inhabitants – only that.

Oki gradually advised Gugenge about various facts that were self-evident truths to a political specialist. One of the bits of advice that attracted Gugenge the most was the construction of a fleet of merchant rafts. His heart was taken by the idea of quitting the current policy of sending one or two rafts to adjacent communities on an adventure, and instead sending a fleet of maybe ten rafts, with protective troops on board, on a long-term tour. It would increase the safety and the profit both, and Gugenge began to research it at once.

Still.

Oki couldn't use his robots very much in this contact with Pijajasta. In addition to the robots' regular duties in the investigation and exploration of Nenegin, they had regular patrols, they recorded the activities of the Nenegia, looked after the Administrator, and maintained protection – in other words, they had their hands full already. In fact, they had a little too much work for their numbers. After the world had progressed a little as a colony, the Federation would supply newer robots, but at the moment they were mostly repaired, readjusted, and sometimes even jury-built. The fact that the robots were intensely loyal to their work – or to their implanted destiny, if one cared to express it that way – also meant that it was extremely difficult to get them to change their work assignments. If Oki merely issued an order to SQ1, it would only give rise to a fault, a weak point in the rigid command structure it topped. Even an expert in robot control like Oki would have to spend a great deal of time adjusting them for the change.

It was the same for this work. Oki could only freely use the relatively high-level robots, and couldn't change the basic priorities of the robot control system.

Sometimes he wondered if it wasn't a little suspicious that things had gone that far. Of course, it was impossible, but he did feel that the robots were not cooperating wholeheartedly with the advance of the Nenegian civilization. One example was the data about Pijajasta. When he had first visited there, SQ1 had reported their average intelligence at 3.41, with the upper one percent at 4.50, and their group effectiveness at nine percent compared to the maximum possible. However, when Oki, amazed at Gugenge's efforts, requested detailed figures, he found that while the upper one percent was 4.50, the upper half percent was 5.25, and the highest tenth of a percent was 5.99. Since the standard report was only for the upper one percent, it had probably been an error on his part not to have asked the robots for more detail. Not only that, but he also knew that the data were about ten years old, and much lower than current values. This problem was one they would address, if he only asked them to. Still, despite knowing the robots' limitations, he remained unhappy about the gaps in their reports.

There were other examples, too.

The robots had known about the buttons being used as high-denomination currency. According to the robots' memory banks, it was standard for items from an advanced culture, even common items, to be highly valued in less-advanced cultures – certainly not surprising. Therefore they had judged it not necessary to tell the Administrator, and had buried it in the data banks. It was just an example of the robots maintaining their devotion to duty by not showering the Administrator with trivial information. At any rate, the previous Administrator had requested this behavior, and Oki hadn't changed the rules.

When he thought about it, he realized that the Administrators were rulers, but only during their term of office. On the other hand, robots were built for one planet, and stayed there until the end. It was only natural that the robots should feel they knew this planet better than the Administrator.

Oki stood up.

He was thinking too much.

Robots didn't have emotions like humans.

"Only five minutes remaining until departure. Please begin your preparations. Only five minutes…" droned SQ2B's voice.

"Welcome! Welcome, and enter! We have been awaiting you!"

After he entered the largest of the several domes the colonists used, and doffed his protective clothing in a brightly-lit room, a couple appeared and greeted him joyously. They were wearing gaudy clothing that made Oki's eyes hurt. The man was wearing a gold breastplate over a richly patterned shirt, and tight pants. On top of that, he had a short-sword on his hip, and a short cape around his shoulders. The woman, had her hair piled up on her head in a feminine style, and was wearing a long-sleeved cream-colored dress, with a thick black cummerbund.

Both of them were wearing dark glasses.

"We are so very pleased you could attend the festivities," said the man again, then turned and called into the next room, "The King has come!"

SQ2A and the two LQ class robots that had accompanied him stopped there. Oki, after dropping his nerve paralyzer gun into his pocket, followed the couple. The area was dark, and Oki had to put on the long-wave glasses he had brought with him. His guides, on the other hand, took off their dark glasses. To them, this blackness was shining in splendid color.

It was an assembly hall. He had only come here once before. Almost two hundred men and women were gathered there, grouped around the scattered tables, whispering and laughing together. Due to the red shift, he couldn't make out detailed patterns or colors, but in any case they wore old-fashioned, brilliant, even wild clothing. Better than "old-fashioned", perhaps, would be to say "anachronistic". They weren't matched, but rather people chose whatever beautiful or rare style from whatever period they fancied, mixing them together.

As he entered, led by the couple, they all turned and applauded.

After waiting for Oki to reach the center table, a hugely fat man raised his arms and signaled for quiet. Oki had met him many times. He called himself the "Prime Minister of the Kingdom of Nenegia".

"The King has come! Let the festivities begin!" he called. "This day is the annual festival for the glory of the Kingdom of Nenegia, and the day for change of Prime Minister. As the custom dictates, the retiring Prime Minister, myself, shall act as host for this party. Thank you. Let us hear the National Anthem!"

72

A prerecorded melody came from the wall speakers, and the massed people began to sing together.

He had forgotten – this man was retiring as Prime Minister – Oki thought while listening to the long "national anthem". Who would be the next, he wondered. Well, whoever it was, they were all the same. After all, there were only about three hundred people here, including the children. They had their own "Kingdom" and "Prime Minister", but it was only a trifling thing.

He suddenly noticed that the singing had ended, and the ex-Prime Minister was facing him, gesturing.

"Sire, we are waiting for your words."

"My words?" said Oki. He recalled that SQI had said it was customary for the Administrator to give an opening address.

"Please," repeated the Prime Minister.

Oki looked at the assembled people. What should he do?

If possible, he should attack their anachronisms, smash their pretences at "royalty", demolish their twisted style of life. He should state clearly that they were not officially recognized colonists, and force them to re-assess their own position. But what was the use of complaining to these isolated people, with no other standard to follow, and no place to go, stranded on this world of visual effects? He would just stir up resentment, and make the next Administrator's job that much more difficult.

At the same time, though, he couldn't fit into their role they had planned for him, as the King of the Kingdom of Nenegia.

There was no helping it – he gave them a standard greeting, wishing them all health, and promising to give full support to their efforts towards building a new society to suit this new world.

They were obviously not pleased with it, but nobody actually criticized him for it. The fact that they had made the Administrator their King indicated that they recognized his authority, and were trying to stabilize their worldview. And so, even if their King did un-Kingly things, they merely adopted the position that he was a strange King, without censuring him. At any rate, that was how it had been up until then.

"Thank you, sire," politely intoned the ex-Prime Minister, and then, raising his glass high, called out "Let us drink to the fourth reigning King, to our noble selves, and to the Kingdom of Nenegia! Kampai!"

They all drank.

At once, the speech of the new Prime Minister began. The thin, sharp-eyed new Prime Minister talked on and on about the beginning of the advancement of the Kingdom of Nenegia due to the efforts of the citizenry, trade with the pig-frogs, and the contributions of the robots – however self-centered they may have been, Oki couldn't very well let them starve, so the robots gave them enough material and manual labor support to keep them at a bare subsistence level – all leading to a new economic and spiritual glory. He went on to praise himself and his Kingdom for incorporating all of the good points of Terra and the other worlds into their culture. It was an awfully boring, long presentation, but the colonists listened to it avidly, not even fidgeting.

Oki let it wash past him. He didn't get upset at their biases and self-defensiveness any more. They could only see the past. They could never imagine or foster new things, different things, things not covered by their custom or habit. What could give birth to these things was the Administrator and the Administrator system…

Really?

Was it really so? The Administrator and the robots were not of the past, but couldn't you say that they were merely trying to maintain the present?

The future… Oki recalled Gugenge and his colleagues. Wouldn't the real future be made by them?

Maybe that was true. After all, wasn't the Administrator system merely an effort by humans to humanize other worlds? However much you quibbled about it…

When the applause flared, he snapped out of it. The speech was over, and the meal was beginning.

Oki put the food in front of him into his mouth. There was synthetic food and processed Nenegian vegetables. There was also something he didn't recognize, with a more solid texture and a strange, meaty taste. He noticed that when he ate it, they smiled at each other with satisfied expressions.

Wasn't this enough already?

Just as he decided to leave, the new Prime Minister approached, bowing.

"I pledge my loyalty, sire," he said. "Still, I, as Prime Minister, must ask for cooperation in certain matters from the King in order to lead our Kingdom to prosperity."

He bowed again.

"As I'm sure you heard from my speech, the political structure of this nation is a rarely-seen ideal form. As the base of the machine-supported King we have the selected nobility who both act as a brake on the King's unilateral actions and give guidance to the natives. A strong bond of friendship exists between the King and the nobility... For this reason, we do not bestow the title of Emperor on the King, and the King does not interfere with the lives of the nobility. In other words, this Kingdom is a nobility with a King, and a King with a nobility."

"..."

An absurd, self-centered logic, though Oki, but he said nothing.

"Both sides have the responsibility to ensure that nothing destroys the relationship of that trust."

The new Prime Minister gradually shed his politeness. "Following this duty, I must counsel the King today."

"Counsel?"

"How is it that the King himself and the pig-frogs have negotiations?"

"..."

"The King should leave all contact with the natives to the nobility. If the need presents itself, then the King should go through his mechanical servants."

"Why should it be that way?"

"The actions of the King towards any group of natives must be same as to all natives. That is, though, obviously impossible, and would lead to contact with only a selected few. It would lead, in other words, to favoritism. The loan of a laser device, coupled with a visit by the King himself, leads to envy from other communities, and undermines the position of the nobility with the natives, that which we have built up with such careful planning."

"…" Oki was amazed, speechless.

"We would like you to cease such contact at once," pressed the new Prime Minister.

"Let me speak." Oki stood up. "Do you truly understand what you are doing?"

"I believe so."

"I don't. I don't believe you understand at all."

Pressed this far, Oki couldn't let it slide. Even if he offended the other a little, he had to make the situation clear. He had to give a clear warning.

"You are seeking to violate the authority of the Administrator appointed by the Federation, and attempting to prevent him from carrying out his orders."

"…"

"It could be interpreted as rebellion against the Federation. I suggest you think about what you are doing – excuse me."

Oki left the speechless Prime Minister and guests behind, and left the hall. As he left, he was not in a good mood.

Hadn't he known it would come to this from the start?

Hadn't he come to the party knowing at the bottom of his heart that he could always brandish his authority as Administrator and wave away any opposition?

When he reached the clothing room, he removed his vision glasses.

He turned… But there was no one following. There was only the dark, smooth blackness.

He slowly put on his protective clothing, and went out into the darkness and rain with SQ2A and the two LQ-class robots.

— 4 —

Dawn.

Even though it was dawn, that wasn't to say that the view from the window became any more blue. There was only a sensation that the darkness had retreated a little into the rain. In any case, there were no windows in this room.

Oki lay on his back, staring at the ceiling. It was too early to get up yet, but his consciousness was already jumping from idea to idea, trying to resist the weight of the surrounding buildings and the black rain. There were thoughts of anger, too.

His heart, which had been light for so long, was becoming blacker and blacker, threatening to be crushed, in these last fourteen or fifteen days. It was not a collapse into despondency as before, but rather the unpleasant tension of things that just don't go right. And the sense of hopelessness towards the cause of it all…

…the colonists, of course.

The words he had thrown at them at the party had set off unexpected ripples. He had expected them to become a little more firm against him, but he hadn't believed that they were stupid enough to actively resist him, as they were doing now.

According to the robots' reports, the colonists had begun to loan lasers to the native inhabitants the morning after the party. Nobody knew how many there were, but a number had been given to communities outside Pijajasta. Oki asked why they were doing so, but only received casually cynical answers, such as "For the advancement of the pig-frogs," and "We learned from the King's actions, and copy him". When he asked them what would happen if the weapons were used for war, they said that the pig-frogs had been told not to do that, and even if they did, then it would merely be necessary to punish them – they repeated his own words, slightly twisted. They said that communities other than Pijajasta had also been requesting laser devices, and the nobility wanted to know why they couldn't profit by responding to the pig-frogs' wishes.

According to the robots, they had done nothing wrong. They were not recognized colonists, and as frontiersmen they had merely done what was customary, and it was nothing to blame them for. Of course, if the Administrator wished to deal with them under his own authority, they would follow his orders, said SQ1.

Oki asked the colonists nothing more. He thought there was no other method but to show them the danger of their own position – and as there was nothing he could do at that point, he decided to wait a little longer and see what developed.

A few days ago, that "a little longer" had become "at once."

Gugenge had come to see him.

Oki didn't remember exactly when it had happened, but he had lost the feeling that Gugenge looked funny. Also, since he had come to know the genius that was Gugenge, he had gained the habit of automatically comparing all other Nenegia to him, seeing Gugenge in them.

Gugenge had managed somehow to build the merchant fleet that Oki had mentioned, and had stopped in at the Administration Complex after a long trading trip to many communities.

Gugenge proudly showed his merchant fleet of forty rafts with trade goods, crew and guard troops to Oki, Oki gave it his approval, and then heard how Gugenge would return to Pijajasta in four or five days, and start intensive work on the laser-produced items – with the laser he had left in Pijajasta, under his assistants' care.

After that, though, Gugenge told him an unexpected bit of horrifying news.

The colonists were using the Nenegia as a food source.

While on their voyage, Gugenge had helped a half-dead Nenegia who had been floating nearby. According to that Nenegia, he and another had gone to the colonists' area to trade, were taken by force, and thrown into a large room covered with metal rope. That room was full of the corpses of Nenegia, and there was a single living Nenegia, in terrible pain and fear. The one they had rescued reasoned that the room was pierced by an invisible poison light, and hid among the corpses. A naked, black-eyed human

78

(in other words, without protective clothing, and wearing sunglasses) came to the room and took away a number of Nenegia, not caring if they were dead or alive. When at last his own turn came, he feigned death, and then kicked his way to freedom half dead. What he had seen there was a view of the corpses of Nenegia being finely cut and cooked. He had managed to escape, but his skin was terribly ravaged and he died soon after in spite of Gugenge's efforts to help him.

Gugenge had one other piece of evidence. He had seen a number of rafts with troops and maybe a dozen other Nenegia on each go to the colonists' area – but when, by accident, he ran into the same group returning later, only the troops remained. Not only that, but those troops called to Gugenge's fleet, and bought a large number of items with the special high-denomination currency. Gugenge didn't believe that all of those Nenegia could have escaped from all of the rafts. Outside their forts, freely-swimming Nenegia would be quickly eaten by the flatfish and soft-bodied predators.

"We would like you to investigate the truth of this," begged Gugenge. "If it true that free Nenegia are being forcibly taken, and either being sold into slavery or eaten, then the Administrator must do something about it."

After that, Gugenge and his rafts left for Pijajasta.

Oki recalled the meat-like dish he had eaten at the party.

Was that… Had that been the flesh of a Nenegia? And when they looked at each other and smiled, had it been their smile of triumph – that they had managed to get the Administrator to eat it? Or maybe it was an attempt to draw him into their group by making him an accomplice to their crime.

In any case, buying a whole Nenegia would be unthinkably expensive under normal trading circumstances. That was why they had introduced the button as the high-denomination trading currency. That was the only possible reason.

Oki ordered the robots to investigate at once. He also told them to carry out the investigation under top-secret status, so as not to notify the colonists of his intent.

SQ1 carried out the order at once.

Proof came to light immediately. The colonists didn't let the robots into their homes, so they couldn't determine exactly what the situation was inside, but a huge number of Nenegia bones were uncovered in the mud near the colonists' settlement, and large amounts of Nenegia flesh fragments were recovered from the sewage system.

The situation was clear. It was unclear if they were being used as slaves, but that they were being eaten was beyond doubt.

The next step was to enter and search the community by force. Then notify the Federation and wait for their judgment. Even though he hadn't noticed it himself, earlier, and even though he had eaten the flesh of a Nenegia himself, he knew there was no help for it.

That was today.

Today he planned to lead the robots into the colonists' settlement. All of the preparations were finished, but... He didn't want to do it. He couldn't help but feel angry at the colonists who had forced him into it. Why hadn't they realized that it would come to this?

Had they really been that simple? Had they really thought that he could permit this? Had they drowned in their color-compensated high-noon world to the point where they became incapable of comprehending?

"Are you awake?" came SQ2B's voice.

"Huh?" Oki focused his eyes.

"SQ1 has an urgent communication. It is not yet time to get up, but as you appeared to be awake, I contacted you."

"What is it?"

"Reporting," said the voice, a little deeper. SQ1 was talking through SQ2B's contact. "A war has broken out among the native inhabitants."

"War?" Oki rose up in his bed. It wasn't that amazing for the Nenegia to fight among themselves. If SQ1 reported it now, then it must be something out of the ordinary.

"Twenty-five minutes ago, LQQ72 on standard patrol discovered two fleets engaged in combat three kilometers north of Pijajasta."

"Pijajasta…?" Oki sprang out of bed.

"The reason I am reporting this is because one side is using laser weaponry. I dispatched SQ2A2 to the scene at once. SQ2A2 will arrive within minutes and begin picture transmission. After you have seen the pictures, please decide if you will refrain from interference as we have up until now, or act."

Lasers?

The Nenegia with lasers?

Without knowing if it was Gugenge or another group that was using them, he dressed and took the elevator to his office.

The office screen was already bright with a black and white moving image.

Two fleets were fighting. No, it wasn't really fighting. The pursuing fleet was firing bright laser beams, and the fleeing side was being destroyed: Nenegia burned, cargo aflame.

"According to the analysis of data received from SQ2A2, the lasers are being used by a combined fleet of several communities. The fleeing group is that of Pijajasta, attempting to return," said SQ1, already in the room.

He understood.

They were being attacked.

Without being told, he understood.

Gugenge's trade fleet was being attacked by other communities that had received lasers from the colonists.

They were probably after the trade goods.

No, wait.

Oki suddenly had a cold thought.

Could it be…?

Would Nenegia really make a combined fleet for that reason? Or… or maybe this was all engineered by the colonists, who didn't appreciate the rapid development of Pijajasta, or the regard that the Administrator had for it. Had they felt their own existence threatened by the union of Gugenge with the Administrator, and so loaned lasers and initiated the use of buttons as high-denomination currency…?

He didn't know.

He didn't know, but it wasn't impossible.

The Pijajasta fleet was scattered to pieces, and the pursuing fleet swept closer.

"There!" shouted Oki suddenly, "Close up on that raft!"

The order was followed at once.

It was the raft Gugenge was riding. It was making all speed to escape the firing range of the other rafts. It would make it.

It was already in front of the main gate of Pijajasta.

"What will you do?" asked SQI.

"..." Oki hesitated for a moment.

It was easy to simply say destroy the lasers. The quickest method was just to make it impossible for the natives to use lasers, as they hadn't yet reached the level of civilization where they could support their own laser devices.

But was that right? They had to pass through many experiences before they could use the tools of civilization properly. For that purpose, shouldn't he let things take their course, and let them settle it in their own way?

And if he made it impossible to use lasers, then Pijajasta could be no exception. Gugenge and his plans for that big step forward in this world...

Giving lasers to the Nenegia other than Gugenge had been a big error. Give a pistol to an idiot, and he might shoot a genius.

He decided in all the turmoil. Gugenge would have to bear it for a while. The reformation would have to advance on its own power, in their own ways. Gugenge could do it, he was sure. Gugenge could do it...

"Intervene! Destroy the laser devices," he shouted.

But it was too late.

Something he hadn't thought of happened. A beam shone from the side of the main gate, from the tower.

Gugenge had left his laser in Pijajasta when he started on the trading trip. That laser pierced through Gugenge's raft, then turned, and began to burn the invading fleet.

By that time, LQQ72 was already destroying the lasers from above, wholesale.

A huge war fleet came out of Pijajasta.

The combined fleet was already retreating. They had lost their lasers, and had no hope of winning against that huge fleet coming to fight them.

The soldiers of Pijajasta… Were different than he remembered.

The *peda*.

They all had many *peda*, some of them dozens of *peda*.

Then Oki understood. It was a coup d'état.

The traditionalists that had wanted to return to the old ways of living had taken advantage of Gugenge's absence to rebel against the reformers. The laser had been placed in the tower for the purpose of killing Gugenge.

The plane flew on towards the site.

Oki was silent, sunken into his seat.

After examining the battle site, he would return to the Administration Complex for a moment, and then go to the colonists' settlement.

It was a hopeless flight.

Gugenge was dead. All of his associates were no doubt executed.

That which Gugenge had almost built was gone, and none would understand it. Nobody understood it, but it should have been the dawn of Nenegin. Now, even if that dawn should come, it had retreated into the distant future. Their bright, distant noon had retreated far, far away.

At the same time, the artificial noon of the colonists was drawing to a close.

For him, thought Oki, for himself, wasn't noon a far distant thing? Here… Here, nothing was permitted a noon.

The sky ahead was purple. Across the purple heavens, the headlight beams shone golden, glittering, lighting up the countless raindrops like a mirage as the flyer pierced through that lavender darkness…

Oki took the vision-restoring spray from his inner pocket, and pressed it to his arm.

The Wind in the Ruins

— I —

Noon must have passed some time ago.

Kazeta ppk Moro set down his work, and walked over to the window.

Today was beautifully clear weather. Again.

And in spite of that brilliant blue sky – or, rather, due to its excessive brightness – he felt the disturbance spreading through him.

Maybe it would be better to take a break.

He approached the door.

As he did, sq2b spoke through the speaker built into the wall: "Are you going out?"

"Mm. Think I'll take a stroll."

"Yes, sir. However, don't you think it would be better to eat your meal first, Administrator?"

"I'll eat later."

"Understood," answered sq2b, and the door opened with a soft click.

He stepped outside.

It went without saying, of course, that the responsibility for his protection shifted at that instant from sq2b, who was responsible for the interior of the Administration Complex, to the mobile chief, sq2a, and at that instant sq2a and his group took up a defensive posture around the Administrator. The central robot, sq1, silently checked and approved their actions.

In his younger days, Kazeta used to be constantly aware of the close interaction between the robots… But that awareness had become a distant thing now. To Kazeta, their relationship was now the same as pushing a button and making a machine move. That was enough, and if knowledge of the mechanism itself was ever required, he had it.

The garden was at the bottom of a wide staircase of white stone.

In the garden, the blossom-grass one saw everywhere was covered in pale crimson flowers, ruffling in the wind. There were small mounds of dewsipper here and there, masses of tiny white flowers. Scattered between them, the neckbrushes hung their semi-transparent blooms, still and helpless.

Kazeta faced into the gentle breeze, and took a deep breath.

There was a sweet, slightly sharp fragrance in the air. On this world, flowers bloomed almost all year round, except in the polar regions, and the multitude of species couldn't be counted. The wind always wafted the aromas of countless flowers, and that delicate harmony changed with each slight variation in wind direction, or temperature, or humidity. Without that constant play and variety, humans would undoubtedly become used to one fragrance in a short time, and couldn't enjoy the full play of smells like this.

No, it wasn't enough to merely say "enjoy". To the people who lived here, the constant, sometimes strong, sometimes subtle, sometimes simple banquet of totally indescribable fragrances mixed together – that ever-changing dream – had become an essential part of their pleasure in life. People recalled their memories through the smells, wrote their imagery. The sense and expression of the fragrances of the air was now firmly bound to all their lives, not only for the dozens of perfume specialists with their sharp sense of smell and analytic ability, or the small number of "artists".

And Kazeta, who had been here seven years, was no exception.

In the wind now was the image of a child's toy, he thought. It quickly melted with the smell of the dewsipper, which recalled metal, and became the memory of his ride on the starship when he had been a cadet specializing in politics, and then finally returned to the overpowering scent of blossom-grass.

Whenever he came across blossom-grass, he always recalled the previous Administrator, Bart. That was probably because Bart had loved it so much. He thought that maybe it wouldn't be correct to say that Bart had loved only the blossom-grass. Bart had loved this planet – had loved all of Tayuneine – and had especially loved the blossom-grass because, to him, it symbolized Tayuneine.

"This world is the last stop for Administrators, you could say," white-haired Bart had commented quietly when he handed authority over to Kazeta.

"Here, everything is oh-so-peaceful, even including the hulks of the native race's ruins. When I first came here, I had been an Administrator on many other worlds, and drove myself to continue to perform here, but... But I lost it before I knew it. Anyway, the only problem here is an occasional spectral visitation, and it's probably the easiest job of any Administrator anywhere. And you change, too, become the same. You come to feel that a relocation to a new world is merely an annoyance. That's why I left the straight and narrow path, and declined to accept my next assignment to another world."

Well, maybe that was so. Not only Bart, but all of the previous Administrators of Tayuneine, with one or two exceptions, had stepped down from their posts as Administrators. The Federation seemed to understand, too, and only sent older Administrators who already had an impressive list of achievements. They were telling you to take a rest, and even to resign should you desire. Of course, whether you did so or not was strictly a matter of personal choice, but you couldn't deny that this place had the feeling of being a "last stop".

Still, the Administrators who resigned after Tayuneine didn't choose to live here. It was most common for them to withdraw to Terra or one of the advanced worlds nearby to enjoy their special citizenship status, awarded for their years of service, or to take up a lower-status, lower-importance job within the Federation bureaucracy. Maybe they couldn't bear being citizens on a world where they used to be the Administrator, being controlled by their own robots... Or maybe it was merely too boring to end their lives in this utopia, for those who knew other worlds of complex vitality... Or yet again, perhaps they wanted to maintain their memories as memories, rather than reliving them as illusions on too-beautiful Tayuneine. In any case, they hadn't elected to stay here as citizens. Bart had thought about staying here, too, but in the end he left with his wife. Bart was one of the few Administrators to be married to a member of the opposite sex in an open-ended contract. If his wife hadn't been from one of the older colony worlds near Terra, then he might well have been the first Administrator to stay on Tayuneine, Kazeta felt. Bart had loved this world that much. Or at least, he had certainly looked as if he had.

The current Administration Complex and the garden had all been built by the robots about fifteen years ago, when Bart had been Administrator. Naturally, that was because the previous structure had become so dilapidated that it couldn't be compared to the colonists' buildings, and although the design had received the formal approval of the Federation, it still strongly reflected Bart's personality. In the size and layout of the garden the reflection of his personal likes was especially strong, and the flowers and shrubs somehow imparted a pleasing impression.

Kazeta began to stroll.

The flowered path gradually rose, and Kazeta crossed the peak of the hill the Administration Complex was built on, continuing towards the forest.

From the top of the hill, he could see Yusa, the largest city on this world – the largest, but it still only had a population of seventy thousand. The buildings of Yusa, scattered among the trees and grass, shone peacefully in the afternoon sun.

But... That scene called forth the shadow in Kazeta's heart that he had forgotten for a time. If he stayed too long, that shadow would become too heavy. He turned towards the shining white Administration Complex, decided to walk a little more, and set off towards the forest again.

Everyone called it a forest, but it wasn't really very big. You could walk through it in fifty minutes, but inside the wind was hushed, and the fragrances changed completely.

He saw something bright and shining move between the trees. From that glance, he was sure it was SQ2A-3. Wherever the Administrator went, SQ2A and its underlings always followed for protection. Bart had instructed the robots to be as inconspicuous as possible, so far as it didn't interfere with their jobs, when the Administrator was thinking like this – and they still loyally followed his command under Kazeta. The robots would never feel self-loathing or stress, no matter how many Administrators they worked for, thought Kazeta, somewhat cynically.

There was a wooden bench under the trees.

He sat down.

Even though he sat, the heaviness didn't leave his heart. Maybe it was uneasiness rather than heaviness. Something had been bothering him for a couple of days now. He knew what it was, exactly.

The Schedule.

An Administrator cadet would come here in one week. After a month of hands-on training, he would leave again, but Kazeta had to evaluate him from his position as Administrator. Although he was called a cadet, he was actually an unassigned Administrator. He had been selected, undergone intensive training and study, and gained qualification as a political specialist – then gone on to choose his specialty, and had again been selected. Finally, he and his classmates would become Administrators if that was their choice, but they were not immediately assigned to work. Before they could be entrusted with their own worlds, they had to tour many worlds to be trained and evaluated by Administrators in the field. If they failed, then they would rise to a different job within the Federation, that of a mere political specialist. In that sense, although they were Administrators on paper, they were still only candidates, cadets.

Kazeta had already trained many cadets on other worlds. There shouldn't be any problems training another here. There shouldn't be any, but it bothered him, strangely.

Why?

The answer, though he didn't want to recognize it, was simple: he wondered if he was still capable of honestly assessing the performance of a cadet.

It had been seven years since he had come to Tayuneine.

Over those seven years he had fulfilled his duty as Administrator. The native inhabitants had become extinct – they estimated it had been several thousand years ago – and there was no other advanced life on this world to trouble the colonists. The colonists themselves were extremely quiet. There were the spectral visitations, of course. Shadows without substance appeared sometimes, and startled people. The colonists firmly believed they were the spirits of the vanished native inhabitants, as did Kazeta himself, but nobody claimed to have proven it yet. But the ghosts had never done any harm except to frighten people, and they weren't his responsibility. The Federation no doubt desired a little stimulation on this all-too-quiet world, and the researchers, whether from this world or others, were neither damaged by the spirits nor able to damage them. Apart from the spectral visitations, there was a phenomenon that had come to be a problem on other worlds – the newer generations of colonists, who didn't know other worlds, had begun to show resentment against the Administrator System – but it had yet to be much of a problem here.

In other words, he could be an Administrator here without too much effort. Not only without effort: he could actually enjoy himself as the months and years passed. Over the years he had lost his fighting spirit and get-up-and-go, just as Bart had done, and the other Administrators before him. He no longer possessed the spirit or habits to let him work on another world. Even if he should desire a new assignment, he realized it would take a tremendous effort on his part.

Was it really acceptable for him to grade the cadet? And not just evaluation, but could he truly train him? If the training were real training, wouldn't he merely pass on his own indolence, which wouldn't befit an Administrator? And if he didn't turn out that way – then he could only think it was because he looked upon the Administrator with scorn, couldn't he?

If at all possible, he wanted to refuse this training. He wanted to say that with so many other colony worlds, it was hardly necessary to bring him here to Tayuneine. It wasn't possible, though, for the Administrator to refuse the assignment. If Tayuneine had been listed on the cadet's schedule, then the Federation must have some plan in mind.

One week later.
That schedule had become a lead weight in his heart.
Not only that.
It wasn't just that a cadet was coming for training.

There was another plan, too.

Samielle PKA Freyn was coming.

And he was coming as a Federation Inspector.

An Inspector.

It was a post initiated under the newly established Inspection System. The Federation had judged that the old methods were no longer adequate to check the Administrators' performance as the number of colony worlds increased, and had added an Inspector who would tour colony worlds and report essential data to the Federation Government. Still, they knew that data collected by people who had only been in the government would be beside the point. Although the highest levels of the Federation realized it might lead to collusion with the local Administrators, they decided, for the time being, to select candidates from among the present Administrators, retrain them, and appoint them as Inspectors.

At the same time, it was also proof that the Federation was beginning to lose the absolute faith in Administrators that it had enjoyed fifty years ago, when the first group was assigned... But, as compensation, they had opened up to the Administrators the chance of obtaining positions as high-ranking Federation officials.

Kazeta knew Samielle PKA Freyn well as a fellow student from the training academy. He was a man of decision, and had managed to tame a number of worlds that had broken other Administrators, starting with Katamin II and Kirienin, which had native inhabitants of high intelligence and military capability.

It was perfectly natural that Samielle PKA Freyn should be appointed Inspector... But not on his world. Inspectors, once they passed down a decision, wouldn't change their mind except under extreme circumstances – they knew no compromise. And any report to the Federation would be in exactly that style... Not anything to be happy about. Not here, not in this condition...

Kazeta opened his eyes. He was still sitting on the bench

The sun spilling through the trees pooled here and there, totally silent. And the standing stones...

93

Those now-indistinct monoliths, half-hidden by the drifting leaves, weathered by the long years of wind and rain, smoothed with moss, but still stones with a definite shape – they peered at him.

Ruins left by the native inhabitants.

A *memento mori* from a species that had become extinct so long ago – long before humanity arrived.

When he saw them, an unexpected sense of peace returned to his breast. He felt he could understand the long, long years that vanished race had waited, and their present eternal rest. The slight irritation he had felt when he first saw their ruins and their artifacts, and realized that humanity, too, would come to this, had vanished at some point. These past two or three years, he had come to feel a strange contentment when he saw them. He didn't know if it was due to him advancing beyond a certain point in life, or maybe he was merely seeking rest when he was tired, but when he gazed on what they had left, and thought of them, a strange tide of peace washed over him.

And.

Mmm...

When he felt that warmth, that emotion, he always felt the presence behind it. Expecting it, he turned around to face what was there.

The shadow.

Wavering, pale green... An "almost" existence, impossible to pin down. A specter. What the people called a "spirit" was there with him.

Even when he looked at it, it didn't retreat. It merely continued to hang there... And began to darken a little, as if to increase the weird sense of familiarity that welled up inside him.

Spirits.

He couldn't explain even to himself why these ghosts that so frightened, even terrified, other people felt so tranquil to him. He couldn't explain it, but he thought it might be because he felt an admiration, a yearning, for that race. Different people saw totally different spirits, but none of them had as gentle a shape or color as that which haunted Kazeta.

The spirit wavered a little longer, and then became fainter and vanished. At the same instant, the sense of peace in his heart vanished. Still, he didn't lose the memory of the tranquility he had felt.

Kazeta smiled quietly to himself. Somehow, he thought the spirit had come to comfort him.

"Thank you, my friend," he whispered softly, and left the bench.

— 2 —

"As per the previously reported schedule, the unassigned Administrator will land at the starport today at four o'clock in the afternoon. I have received confirmation," said SQ1.

"Right," nodded Kazeta.

Of course SQ1 was using Tayuneine time. SQ1 had revised the time reported from the way-station planet, which had been in Sol Standard, to local time. As Sol Standard had absolutely no meaning on other worlds, it was only used in formal communications and directives. Tayuneine, along with many other worlds, used Terran hours as time units. As there were no native inhabitants, the colonists had used whatever time units they had brought with them, and there had been total confusion at the start. The person in charge at that time (a Federation Forces officer, as the Administrator System hadn't been established yet) had made Terran time the convention on his own authority. However, as Tayuneine had neither the same year nor day as Terra, one day had become twenty-six hours, and one year had thirteen months, including two months with twenty-eight days, in addition to having a minor leap year every other year and a major leap year every four years. A number of Administrators had tried to rationalize the system, but the colonists had proven unexpectedly conservative, and had overwhelmingly favored leaving things as they were – and so the system remained irrational.

Four o'clock in the afternoon meant the sun would still be up. He thought it would be good to go and meet him.

"All preparations, including the dormitory, have been completed for his use. SQ2D and his section will see to his needs during his training period here," continued SQ1. "Do you have any other directives?"

"Let me see ... "

Just as he was about to ask SQ1 to make preparations to go meet the unassigned Administrator – the cadet – SQ1 began talking.

"Excuse me, but LQ1 has just made contact. There is a request from Yusa City."

"What is it?"

"I will summarize LQ1's data. Today predawn there was an optical phenomenon across an significantly large sector of Yusa City…" – SQ1 corrected itself, perhaps recalling that Kazeta had said that even though robots couldn't sense it, it hadn't been proven to be an illusion – "… in other words, a spectral visitation. According to our sources, the City Council opened a meeting at the request of those who saw the disturbance two hours ago to discuss the phenomenon, and decided to ask the Administrator to attend and explain how he intends to deal with it. This request was submitted to an LQ-class robot five minutes ago."

"… again…" muttered Kazeta.

This kind of request came without fail two or three times a year from one city or another. It was the second time that Yusa City had made the request since he had become Administrator. The spirits were constantly appearing, and rarely became a problem because there were only one or two people involved, and a City Council meeting wasn't held unless it was a massive problem. But… When a large number of people were plagued by unusually terrifying spirits at the same time, the City Council couldn't ignore it either, although that just meant running to the Administrator with their tails between their legs, unable to think of any good policy themselves. Of course, they knew from experience that the Administrator could do no more than they could on their own, but whipped by the people, they were left with no choice. The root of the matter was that the Administrator controlled the robots, and had absolute power over them all, judging all inter-city problems. Even their Administrator, though, couldn't make the spirits vanish, and when requested could only listen to the reports, promise to investigate the causes as much as possible, and, when no results were forthcoming, try to convince them that worlds as suitable as this one were very rare, and they would just have to put up with minor problems like spirits. And the people, even if not totally convinced, still adopted the attitude that this was the way things were, and became quiet and returned to their work until the next disturbance.

It was, to be blunt, a ritual. A play.

That fact should be well-understood by colonists over a certain age, because this problem happened every ten or fifteen years in every city, and it was those too young to remember the earlier disturbance, or those who had forgotten it, who opened the city meeting.

Still... Kazeta frowned. Following that cycle, this disturbance at Yusa was too early. The last time had been the year after his assignment, and only six years had passed since then, which meant that it was probably a disturbance on a massive scale, or that there were new conditions that hadn't been present before.

"Will you attend the Yusa City Council meeting?" asked SQI.

"I'll go. Make preparations," returned Kazeta. If he said he wouldn't go, then SQI would relay that to LQI, and LQI, who was in charge of the observation and protection of the colonists, would take steps to prevent any problems from occurring. He had, though, no reason to refuse, and it was best to take every opportunity of this type to meet with the colonists. Plus which, he had an interest in why Yusa should issue such a request after only six years.

"Preparations for the trip to Yusa have been initiated," said SQI after a pause of about two seconds, and spoke again after another slight pause. "Do you have any instructions concerning the unassigned Administrator?"

"...Oh, yes..." recalled Kazeta.

He had planned to go greet him himself, hadn't he?

If he went to Yusa, though, there wouldn't be enough time. Well, what the hell.

"I am awaiting your instructions," pressed SQI.

"No, no instructions," answered Kazeta.

Yusa was a beautiful city.

The widely spaced homes and buildings had parks and plazas, white roads and ponds reflecting the sky between them, full of natural green and buried in varicolored flowers.

Not only Yusa, of course. Whichever city you might name on Tayuneine, each had its own unique beauty. It was only natural, here where there were no dangers such as wild animals, and where high technology and advanced materials were available to a small population in a fertile environment.

The people living here in these cities were warm and pleasant, and had astonishingly fewer quarrels than people did in similar cities on other worlds. To be more precise, no one except that sort of tranquil person could stand to live there. In the early period of colonization, there had been a number of people with combative personalities or the lust for power, but there was nothing for them to do on this world. Here – where the fragrances of the flowers talked, where tilling the soil and harvesting fruit filled the days, the people playing together, with all their other needs supplied by the robots – those early settlers hadn't been able to stand it. If this had merely been a peaceful Eden, they would have organized the people, created wealth and rank and sought to grasp power at the apex, striving for it. But… There had been robots here from the first, with instructions to crush any movements of that sort, and the robots never missed. To fulfill themselves, those aggressive people had turned to the more competitive worlds near Terra, or to the colony worlds on the frontier.

At the same time, there were many people who heard of Tayuneine, and came, by some accident, to be enthralled by its beauty, and to migrate there. Of course, a large percentage finally elected to become permanent residents… The current Administration Complex welcomed them happily, waited for them to settle down in some city, and supplied robot labor to construct their buildings. The cities didn't always welcome new citizens. They had their own rules – such as a trial period to make sure there were no problems with the newcomer, or the need for sponsorship by some number of city residents – or they merely watched to see how the immigrants fit in. When people couldn't fit in where they wanted to, the Administrator had to recommend another location. And the rich ground of Tayuneine was still wide and open, unaffected by any population increase.

The car carrying Kazeta and sq2a proceeded towards the City Hall of beautiful Yusa, in the eastern region. Even though it was the Administrator's car, it wasn't a long-distance car. It was a handsome car; it even had windows... And it was only accompanied by the lqq7 car carrying sq2a-2.

However, Kazeta's car stopped before it reached the main door.

One of the city people had come out to greet him.

As Kazeta had privately expected, it was Raine, the City Hall Manager.

She came running over to the car at once. The robots, knowing she was harmless from previous encounters, gave way, though they stayed alert for other possible dangers.

"It's been a long time. How've you been?" she asked in a small voice as Kazeta got out.

"Pretty busy. I wanted to call you, but... I didn't really have anything to say... How are you?"

She shrugged in response.

"As well as could be expected. Not all that well, I guess. Ahh... Had a lot of work here, too."

She looked Kazeta straight in the face.

"You came at once today. I thank you on behalf of the people of Yusa City. They're waiting. If you'll come with me, Administrator," she said, and began to walk ahead.

Kazeta hesitated for just a moment, then followed after Raine with the robots.

The City Council Hall was overfull, and the men and women were shouting something at the Council members on the stage. When they noticed Kazeta's arrival, they all fell silent, following his progress with their eyes. By the time Kazeta ascended the platform, a deathly silence held sway.

Kazeta was tense. He had been to many Council meetings in many cities, but this was the first time he had encountered this atmosphere. When the Administrator made an appearance at a City Council meeting, he was usually greeted with either applause or polite bows.

Today was different.

What was going on?

As he and Raine were settling down in the chairs offered to them, he tried to assess what had happened by reading the people's faces. There was no indication of enmity on the faces of the men and women turned his way. It didn't seem to be the "don't come here" attitude of the younger generation towards the Administrator, either.

What was it?

He didn't know.

He didn't know, but as the veteran Administrator he was, he didn't make any slip that would let them know he was lost. Administrators, regardless of how lost they might be, didn't reveal it in even a single muscle of their faces. Especially in this situation, where he didn't know what might begin to happen, he had to show the same blank expression as the robots behind him.

The head of the City Council stood up.

"As the Administrator has now arrived, I would like you to relate the events of this morning once again."

The men and women in the hall began to stand up one at a time in response to his summons, and retold their experiences. In general, things took this form when there was a disturbance. The people who had seen the spirits wanted to express how terrified they had been to the people around them. As they were so used to expressing the delicacies of the fragrances of the atmosphere to each other, their expressions were vivid, and the scenes of that morning came to life brilliantly... Of course, there was also a tendency to exaggerate, so he had to discount their stories slightly.

Still.

As he listened to the unceasing flow of experiences, even from that point of view, he noticed that the situation was not simple.

Usually the shapes seen by people all varied, were all different. When many people saw the same vision at the same time, they revealed many differences under questioning.

This time, though, they had all seen the same thing.

"I saw it too!" shouted a thin old man, leaping up. "Me, too, I saw it too! It's no lie, Mr. Administrator, Sir. At dawn... In my home, standing in the kitchen. It was about a meter tall. I had just gotten up to get a drink of water, and I tottered and fell. My daughter came at the sound when I fell, but... She froze when she saw the ghost. Then it spoke. 'Depart. Leave this world,' it said, then went through the wall and outside."

"And what form did it have?" asked a councilor.

"The same as they all say," he panted. "Those extinct natives of Tayuneine... Uh, right. Just like that famous picture they draw, based on the scientists' research. And it had angry eyes."

Mmm...

All the stories were the same. All of them said they had seen images of the original inhabitants of this world.

Kazeta had, of course, seen that famous picture – quite some time ago, the scientists had come here, and painted it based on recovered bone fragments and ruins and artifacts they had located. According to their theories, the natives had been about a meter tall, like a horned owl with two arms, and seemed to have possessed a civilization totally different from that of humanity. Since then, many had studied the native inhabitants, but none had yet challenged that original hypothesis.

Specters exactly like the hypothetical picture had appeared all across the eastern side of Yusa City.

"After hearing these stories, you must all be aware that this is of a totally different nature from the visitation of six years ago", said the Council Chairman after the retelling was finished, facing half the audience but speaking to Kazeta.

"In other cities as well, I have never heard of a disturbance across such a large area, and all with the same appearance. Do you know of any other example similar to this?"

"No," answered Kazeta, left with no other choice.

"We have come to believe that the visions that appear and vanish on Tayuneine are the ghosts of the native inhabitants," the Council Chairman continued slowly. "The... hatred, perhaps? Well, at any rate, the thoughts of that race that lived thousands of years ago still remain. No, it has never been proven, but that is what we believe. But… today is the first time I've ever seen them in their actual forms."

"…"

"What is your opinion concerning this?"

"Mm. At the moment, I can't say very much."

"We have been discussing the problem since this morning," said the Chairman. "Our conclusion is… We have somehow angered the spirits of the native race."

The hall quieted again until you could hear a pin drop.

"What exactly do you mean?"

When Kazeta spoke, the people began to make a little noise.

"You have no idea?"

"None."

The people fidgeted even more than before.

"In that case, although it may border on being rude, I will inform you," said the Chairman, shifting his gaze directly to Kazeta. "We have heard a rumor. That rumor is… That a number of people will come to Tayuneine from the Federation."

"A number of people?"

"That another Administrator will come, or that a high Federation official will come…"

"That is not a rumor."

Kazeta forced himself to speak placidly. "It's a fact… And the appropriate people were so informed from the beginning, and it has been publicly announced."

"Exactly."

"It looks to me as though you have misunderstood it."

Kazeta spoke in a light voice, but none of the listeners showed it in their expressions.

"An Administrator will come, but he is an unassigned Administrator, or merely a cadet, if you prefer that term. He will come for training. The Federation official is an Inspector." He could not express his apprehensions as to what Samielle PKA Freyn might do. "The Inspector has merely come to see if this world is going well or not."

"I wonder..."

"Excuse me?"

"Would those people come here for that? One Administrator is enough for Tayuneine. It's been that way in the past, and it should work fine in the future. And now two people from the Federation... No, probably many people in the future. And if they send so many people, isn't their goal to change Tayuneine?"

"..." Kazeta was silent. Rather than reply, he thought it was time to listen to what the other had to say.

"That is what I meant by rumor," grumbled the Chairman. "That the Federation wants to change things."

"..."

"From the viewpoint of the Federation, this world is too fruitful, and too lacking in development – and that's true. But we like it this way. We don't want to become a lively world, a world that changes every day."

"I understand that completely."

"And don't the spirits of the native race also want to stop changing? They that vanished and had been sleeping peacefully haven't quietly accepted our invasion thus far, have they? That's why they appear every so often... And if the Federation, like it so often does, turns things upside down, then it's understandable they should get angry. They have begun to drive out all humans. That's what we think! Isn't that right?"

"Right!" shouted a single voice, and all the others took it up.

Then, applause.

After the applause ended, the Chairman continued.

"Of course, this is not your fault. But you, as Administrator, can alter the course of the Federation, can't you? For the spirits of the natives, sleeping... And for us, can't you exert your power? This is what we beg of you."

"Please!"

"Help us!"

"Please!" shouted the people, many people.

"You are making a grave error," said Kazeta, cutting out one word at a time, silencing their shouts with his hand. "At least, that is the only conclusion that I can draw at this moment. As Administrator, I have access to much more data than you, and according to that data, there's no way they could be planning to change Tayuneine."

"You lie!" shouted a young man on the right end of the front row.

"Listen to me." Kazeta sharpened his tone. "I love this Tayuneine, as do you, just as it is now. Let me state that very clearly. I want to add this. You are imagining things, and misunderstanding the Federation. That is what I think, but I promise you that I will exert every effort within my power to prevent the situation you fear. That I promise."

They cheered.

The Chairman clasped Kazeta's hand, and shook it wildly.

Kazeta and the robots descended the platform, and slipped out of the City Hall, led by Raine. This time the long, long handshakes continued until they finally reached the outside.

"Thank you."

Watching the Chairman and the other members of the City Council who had come out to see him off, Raine whispered quickly. "I knew you'd promise them that."

"You're all just jumping to conclusions, you know."

"I wonder. Then why did they all appear in that form? And..." Raine started to speak, and stopped suddenly when the Chairman and the others appeared. Not only the Chairman, but everyone in the city pressed forward towards him, and the robots trying to protect him were busy scurrying back and forth.

He finished his goodbyes, exchanged a glance with Raine on the other side of the human fence, and climbed into his car.

When would he meet her again, he wondered?

He looked at his watch. It was past five in the afternoon.

The cadet had already landed at the starport, and been led to the Administration Complex by the robots.

The cadet – and later the Inspector, Samielle PKA Freyn.

He wasn't likely to have the spare time to meet Raine for a while.

Not for a while.

Not until the cadet and the Inspector left…

He opened the car window.

Countless strong fragrances enveloped him at once. As always, they changed quickly to one he remembered, and called forth a vivid memory.

A memory.

A memory of the ruins.

It was a memory of one small ruin in particular, among all the hundreds on Tayuneine.

Yes, yes, that memory…

It was the ruin he had walked through with Raine on official business.

I'd like to go there again, he thought. I want to go to that tiny ruin again, together with her.

Suddenly…

He felt his heart grow mellow. More than the lightness he felt thinking of Raine, a much more expansive, softer, defending presence was there.

The shadow.

Next to him, inside the Administrator's car, at the side of SQ2A, wavered that ever-so-gentle pale green shadow.

"Here!" he thought, and fell into that peaceful land. As he crossed over, he looked at the shadow, and felt the familiar longing for that vanished race come bubbling up.

He felt like he had heard a song. The song of peace of that extinct people… Not an angry voice, nor a deluded screaming, but a song that would lead to the peaceful land, a song that you couldn't quite catch the words of, no matter how hard you tried. Maybe not a song, but a thought. A shapeless, silent thought…

The shadow vanished.

He sank into his seat deeply, still silent. He had never let it be known to others how the spirits that terrified them so much had such a gentle face for him. Not even to Raine. It could lead to no good end to have it said that the Administrator liked the spirits.

"Do you feel ill?" asked SQ2A.

"No," he answered.

Now that he thought about it, there was no need to tell the robots about it at all. After all, they couldn't see the spirits.

— 3 —

The instant he returned to the Administration Complex, SQ1 told him that the unassigned Administrator had already arrived and was waiting for him. The reason that SQ1 hadn't informed him while he was returning was that everything was proceeding on schedule, and the Administrator hadn't asked. Since he would find out as soon as he returned anyway, SQ1 had judged that there was no need for a special announcement. Of course, from the viewpoint of SQ2D, who was responsible for the unassigned Administrator, Kazeta should have been informed at once, but SQ1 had stopped that. One of the main duties of SQ1 was to process as much as possible at the robot level, and to cut out unnecessary data so as not to disturb the Administrator.

"And that cadet, uh, unassigned Administrator, is not waiting in the room you assigned him?" asked Kazeta.

"No. He is waiting for you in the Administrator's Office."

"The Office?"

"Yes. According to SQ2D, he expressed that desire."

"Hmm…"

It was so much more comfortable to wait for the Administrator's directives in a private room. It was a strange cadet who would go out of his way to wait for him in his office.

When he entered his office, the small-framed man sitting across from SQ2D turned, then rose and came to meet him.

"Administrator Kazeta? I'm Thomas PPKE Jackson. Pleased to meet you."

"My pleasure."

As he responded, Kazeta noticed that the other was unusually old.

He had known the name of the unassigned Administrator who was to come here through the assignment system, but they had refused to tell him anything of the other's age or past history. It hadn't been that way in the past, but now they said they only sent the person's name. They said they wanted the training to be as fair as possible, and for the Administrator to have no preconceptions. Since he could find out easily enough just by asking the cadet, it seemed a little strange to go to such lengths... The central body of the Federation had grown too big, too complex, and was finally starting to flow along purely formal currents... There were more than a few examples of it ignoring the facts of a situation. In any case, that was why Kazeta knew only the name of the cadet coming to Tayuneine, and had unconsciously assumed, based on past experience, that the cadet would be a young man, possessed by his duty.

But the man in front of him now was not like that. He was maybe five or six years younger than Kazeta, but by no means a young man.

Probably this cadet Thomas had fallen behind the others for some reason, or had, as others had, been a specialist in politics or some other field and had transferred on his own initiative or the Federation's order.

Even so, Kazeta had no choice but to treat him the same as any other cadet.

He spoke.

"I had intended to greet you... But there was a problem."

"No matter. Don't worry about it. It's not as if it's an official duty of the Administrator to go and meet unassigned Administrators."

"..."

Kazeta looked at the other's face. What Thomas seemed to be saying, and what his voice revealed were a little different. Somehow, this cadet seemed to feel his pride had been hurt. It looked like he'd been stuck with a noisy one, this time.

Even so – Kazeta noticed the room had a slightly different feeling than usual. Somehow hard to breathe. When he saw the windows, he understood – he always left them open, but now they were tightly closed.

He started to walk towards them, to open them up.

"Uh... If it's not any trouble, could you leave them closed?" asked Thomas.

"Why?" asked Kazeta, stopping his hand.

"I get a headache from it," Thomas grimaced. His expression was a bit too obvious for someone who was likely to become an Administrator.

"In this air, there's something... It's saturated with the smell of flowers or something, right? Somehow I just can't... "

" ... "

If that were the case, then there was no help for it. Kazeta faced Thomas and sat down.

"Each planet has its own special characteristics," he said. "This Tayuneine is no exception. If you're going to undergo training here, you're going to have to get used to it."

Thomas smiled strangely.

"But... Isn't this planet special?"

"What do you mean?"

"The Administrators who come here... This is hard to say, but... "

"Say it."

"I've heard that all of the Administrators that come here become – satisfied with their situation. In other words... Don't get upset, but they say that Administrators all fail here."

"... I see."

"I think I can understand the reason. The smell. The smell of Tayuneine. You all become drunk on it, and lose your ambition."

Thomas gained confidence, and continued.

"That's why I've decided to avoid smelling this atmosphere as much as possible..."

"..." Kazeta was silent for quite a long time.

Failure, he had said.

The phrase "last stop", that Bart had used, echoed in his heart. Of course, this Administrator could only interpret it in that way.

Still.

What of it?

As long as Tayuneine was included in the map of the Federation, someone had to be Administrator there.

Now, it was him.

And now that Administrator had accepted a cadet... If he just treated everything that way, it would be all right.

Kazeta grabbed hold of himself, and asked a question.

"Before you came here, where else did you train?"

"This is the first. After this, I'm to go to Rendolune and Luxerne," answered Thomas, looking curiously relieved.

"Rendolune... I served there for three years," nodded Kazeta. "At that time, it was a standard frontier-stage colony. Now they've made land treaties with the native inhabitants, and industrialized the human territories."

"That's right."

"I don't know Luxerne very well."

"It's a new colony world in system 1325," explained Thomas. "A Class III, Type 0 world, and the native inhabitants seem to be going well, too."

Including Tayuneine, all of those worlds are doing well, thought Kazeta, and nodded instead of saying it aloud.

"And after that?"

"That's all."

"Only three? In my time, we had to go around to at least twelve worlds of varying types."

"Yes, but I'm only going to three," repeated Thomas. The same brazenness he had shown at the start appeared again. "The Federation decided on three, so three is enough, right?"

He talks just like a member of the Federation central body, thought Kazeta. Thomas just wouldn't fit the mold of other cadets in Kazeta's memory.

"Tell me a little about the disturbance you mentioned before – another spectral visitation?"

"Uh-huh, that's right. You asked the robots?"

"Yes. But it was not easy trying to pry information out of them," he said cynically. "Are these robots under some special order? They don't seem to be too interested in serving an unassigned Administrator."

"What do you mean by that?"

"Well, it's true, isn't it? The main chief, SQ1, merely falls silent and refuses to answer my questions, and SQ2A doesn't even answer my call –

and it's supposed to be your outings chief, according to the robot organization chart. I was forced to call the SQ2D assigned to me here, and question it."

"Naturally."

"What?"

"You are misusing the robots. Of course SQ1 and SQ2A will not respond to your directives."

"But SQ1 is the overall-in-charge for this world... "

"SQ1 has responsibility only to the Administrator. SQ2A is under SQ1, so as far as a cadet is..."

"Formally, unassigned Administrator."

"OK. Anyway, the entire robot complement of any world is controlled by SQ1, which is under the control of the Administrator. Only the Administrator can give this network orders. Unless unassigned Administrators are given special authority, they are outside the chain of command. You can only control the section controlled by SQ2D, and even that is subject to the control of SQ1."

"Oh, I see."

"It would have been better if you'd stayed in your room. As long as you stay there, SQ2D will meet all of your needs. For you, SQ2D serves the same role as SQ1, but is not, of course, in contact with the other robots."

As he spoke, Kazeta felt his anger rising. Why hadn't this cadet been taught these things when he went through training?

Was this what they called a cadet?

Was this what they called an unassigned Administrator?

Well, he probably had the literal qualifications. That was why the Federation had sent him, but... Was this performance now acceptable for an Administrator?

And in spite of only having such a small smattering of knowledge, he had entered the Administrator's Office alone, tried to control the robots, and wasn't even reflecting on his own actions now.

When Kazeta had been a cadet, under the first Administrators such as Kurobe and Rainan, this kind of thing couldn't have been imagined. Even a minor miss had been recorded as a major demerit. Even his friend and classmate Kalgeist Jr., who had achieved such brilliant success during training, had finally had to give up his dream of becoming a cadet because of a failure in field training. Not just his own past, but the cadets he had received on other worlds had actually possessed ability, and had respected the limitations of their own positions. Had things really changed this much in the past ten years?

"I understand. I'll study harder."

Thomas somehow understood what Kazeta was thinking, and relaxed. He started his earlier conversation again.

"But about these spectral visitations... I wonder..."

"What?"

"Do the people living here really believe in spirits and things?"

"..."

Kazeta didn't understand what the other was trying to say at first.

"In other words," said Thomas, shaking his head, "The people here believe that the spirits really exist and appear by their own volition. That's what they think, right? In spite of it being only an optical phenomenon."

"Is it?"

"Of course it's only a visual effect. It can't be detected by the robots, so it can't exist. I studied a bit about this planet before coming here. I learned a little more from SQ2D today, and I think I've figured out the real situation here."

"Really? Please, do tell."

"Even if it's not a particularly astonishing opinion, it is my own. It's not especially different from what many others have said... It's just an illusion born from the minds of the people."

"Why do you suspect this?" pressed Kazeta, though of course he knew this theory well.

"Well, there are many ruins from the original inhabitants here on Tayuneine, so the colonists began to feel eyes behind them. After all, this world wasn't a human world, at first. Living here, they gradually came to feel that it was somehow bad, and that thought became an illusion that ghosts were appearing. You can explain it all psychologically."

"I see. But this isn't the only world that has had native inhabitants. So why is only Tayuneine plagued with spirits?"

"That's easy. Haven't the people here become used to living easily in peace together? That's why they see illusions and become terrified at trivial psychological pressures. In other words, they're over-protected."

"According to your theory, people who are not colonists, for example the two of us, should never see these spirits."

"Of course. We're not mentally sterilized. Wait a minute... Surely you're not scared of these ghosts, too?"

"I'm not frightened of the ghosts."

"Right. We're different from the native inhabitants and the colonists, because we're standing on the side of the government."

At that statement, Kazeta felt yet again that the other was not an Administrator.

"I've been thinking," said Thomas. "If we respond to each and every colonist's complaint, then these disturbances will continue forever, right? To dispel their self-indulgent illusions, we should use a more forceful..."

"I'm the Administrator."

Kazeta stood up.

"I am governing this world as ordered by the Federation as a Class IV, Type s2 world. Under that method of government, the amount of individual decision permitted the Administrator is great, but I will not accept your directives... Return to your room and rest. We'll be busy from tomorrow."

"Yes, sir."

Thomas left.

After he left, Kazeta threw open the windows. The fragrances of the night came rushing in, totally different from those of the day. He breathed them into his lungs deeply... But his heart didn't lighten at all.

From tomorrow, he had to progress with Thomas' training in addition to his regular duties.

114

Training meant finding out exactly how much politics he had learned, exactly how well he could respond to the needs of a real colonial world. Even so, though, it was dangerous to entrust an entire world to this inexperienced man, so it meant allowing him to deal with only carefully limited problems. Cadets first saw how to handle robots by observing the Administrator, and constantly compared their methods, sticking as close to him as possible and striving to breathe in tune with him. At last, the cadet would govern under strict control, using his assigned robots as if they were the entire robot complement of the world. The Administrator would, in turn, watch and test him from the start, forcing him to study areas that were insufficient, gradually leaving more and more to the robots, finally only meeting with the cadet occasionally while listening to reports from SQ2 and giving whatever directives might be needed. Still, any bad effects caused by the actions of the cadet were his responsibility, so he had to pay attention, close attention.

Especially when that cadet was, like Thomas... a pain.

Much as Kazeta had feared on that first night, Thomas' ability was far below the minimum. True, he had some degree of knowledge and technique, but when you pressed for more, it all got pretty hazy. In particular, his basics weren't clear. Sometimes he would dash out the right answer immediately, but at other times he would be at a loss, floundering in totally unrelated areas.

Even so, Kazeta continued to earnestly teach the cadet – Thomas continued to refer to himself as the unassigned Administrator. If Kazeta had been the Administrator of one of the more difficult worlds, he probably wouldn't have had the time or interest. He sometimes felt that the Federation had seen Thomas' inability, and that was why he had been assigned to Tayuneine... But Thomas worked hard, managed to learn how to handle the robots, learned the tricks of the trade, and even stopped showing his distaste for the atmosphere.

To say that Kazeta had started to feel a sense of good will towards him was wrong – it was just the opposite. Thomas became more disagreeable with every passing day. Thomas' personality was simply unacceptable.

His willingness to draw the name of the Federation like a sword, his prejudice towards native inhabitants and colonists, his terrifying habit of deciding things on his own, his pushiness when explaining his own opinions… Kazeta just couldn't accept his way of thinking or his attitude. He couldn't accept it, but he couldn't let it affect his objectivity. Kazeta kept guiding Thomas, supported by his strong sense of duty, one of the special characteristics of an Administrator.

Still.

He couldn't become entangled in Thomas only. This training was merely an extra, and his real work was still the government of Tayuneine.

And Tayuneine was increasingly in turmoil.

Shortly after Thomas had arrived, the spirit disturbances began to accelerate.

They weren't the same as before, either. The same thing that had happened at Yusa City – the appearance of the natives themselves crying "Leave this world!" – began to occur in many other areas as well.

At the same time, the rumors that he had heard in Yusa – that the native inhabitants were angered at the machinations of the Federation, plotting to develop and energize this world – it spread from city to city like the plague, whispered from mouth to mouth.

Still, at that point, it seemed that the people hadn't lost their trust in the Administrator, and many cities begged him to attend their City Council meetings and explain if the Federation really intended to do such a thing or not. He always responded to their requests, saying that it was a rumor with no basis in fact, that they should be calm, and that he was also against any change on this world. He couldn't cancel Thomas' training, so he cut his sleep time short, squeezing in extra hours to teach him – and many were the times that Thomas complained about training at such odd hours. But Kazeta felt there was still a great deal of worth in visiting the cities, calming the citizens.

And then.

A message came in that the Inspector would arrive in one week.

Kazeta was at a loss as to whether he should publicly announce this fact as he always did. If he announced it, people would become excited, and there was certainly no obligation to do so. On the other hand, if he didn't, and people found out somehow, then their suspicions would become certainties. If Inspector Samielle PKA Freyn came unannounced, and they knew of it, then someone would explode, maybe in front of the Inspector himself. In the end, he publicized it all in good grace.

As he had known they would be, the reactions of the people were fierce. This world was, they said, the target for the Federation's reconstruction after all. Rumors spread that the current Administrator didn't have the power to stop it, or worse, was actually working with the Federation to deceive them. SQI relayed a number of such reports to him, but the robots must have been collecting many thousands more.

The number of spectral visitations rose dramatically. Almost every city had one every night, and the terrified people would throng the streets wailing.

At last, they stopped asking the Administrator for help. They had come to believe that he was merely a tool of the Federation.

As Administrator, though, Kazeta couldn't let the situation go. City functions were becoming paralyzed, people were terrified. He led his robots from city to city, forcibly arguing that the Federation had no such plans, that the visitations must be for another reason, and that the true reasons would become clearer with time.

It had no effect.

They were already terrified of the ghosts. In addition to the other rumors, one started that the end of the world was coming. The native inhabitants had seen through the Federation's schemes, and rather than let development ruin their eternal sleep, they had decided to destroy the world, ruins and colonists together. Kazeta kept trying to convince them, but there was no help for it. He kept trying, though it seemed hopeless.

The Inspector would arrive on Tayuneine early the next morning – and it was dawn now.

"Any effect?" came Thomas' voice as Kazeta finally returned home exhausted. "Why don't you quit, stop this useless effort?"

Without waiting for Kazeta's answer, he gave a thin laugh, and continued.

"They won't even listen to you now. They're all saying 'To the Ruins! To the Ruins!'"

"I know," replied Kazeta in a low voice.

It was true.

Who started it he didn't know, but, in this last day or two, the colonists were leaving their homes and setting out for the ruins as if possessed. To them, as they could no longer believe in the Administrator, they needed something to rely on, and had turned right around, turned to the ruins, and to the spirits of the native inhabitants. They sat in the ruins, stretching out their arms, entreating them to help, entreating them to stop the Federation from doing this.

It was a strange psychology... Maybe it was only a natural development for the colonists. To them, this world was home. When they feared that they would perish along with their home's destruction, they had chosen the supernatural forces of their homeland over the Federation and the Administrator.

"Peasants. Idiots."

Thomas laughed.

"Nothing's going to happen even if they go to the ruins – they're scared of the illusion they're making themselves. They don't understand that if they just stop believing, the ghosts will stop appearing."

"..."

"They're all dancing to the pipes of their own illusions. They say that the Inspector is coming, and then powerfully imagine these ghosts. So they have the appearance of the native inhabitants – so what? That picture was painted by scientists, right? Does anybody really know if they looked like that or not? And if you think of the way they appear, it's even clearer. The frequency increases with each announcement, each time a visitor comes from outside. If it's not psychological, then what is it?"

"..." He's repeating the same hypothesis again and again, thought Kazeta silently.

Or maybe they really were just psychological disturbances, like Thomas said. Or at least, you could explain a lot of it that way.

But if that were true, then what did Kazeta see every two or three days now? Was that an illusion, too? Was the peace the shadow imparted to him an illusion, too?

He couldn't believe it, but... He didn't offer any counter-arguments. Lately he had stopped arguing with Thomas, except when necessary. It only made him angry.

"If you see things like that, it just shows your suggestiveness and your lack of mental freedom. As proof, healthy people... We don't see them."

Thomas suddenly looked straight into Kazeta's eyes.

"Why? Administrator Kazeta, why are you so soft on them?"

"Soft?"

Kazeta returned his gaze, piercingly.

"That's right. Since I've come here, I've been watching the way you work. You're a highly able Administrator, but I think you're a little misguided. You're too soft on them. To say it bluntly, you're flattering them, playing up to them."

"Do you have any idea of what you're saying?"

"Yes, I think so. Your evaluation of me is going to be terrible, so whatever I say from now on won't make it any worse. You should discipline them until they don't have the time to play at seeing visions. You should drive out these illusions, wake them up, even if you have to kill a hundred of them, or two hundred. You should develop this sleeping planet, completely, and smash those ruins."

"So this is the real you." Kazeta approached one step. Thomas retreated one step, and continued to howl.

"The reason you don't do it is because you've become too much of Tayuneine. You're drenched, drowned in this world!"

"Listen, you."

Kazeta grabbed the other's shirt front. He had lost his self-control as Administrator. "Just where the hell do you think you are? Tayuneine! You think you can be a real cadet, when you abuse your own world like that?"

"I don't care about your damn evaluation! It doesn't have any meaning in my case!" shouted Thomas. "I've had enough. It's because people like you exist that this world is accepted, is a member of the Federation!"

"..."

Kazeta dropped his hands. When he argued with this man, and lost even a little self-control, he was not proud of it.

Thomas fell backwards, sat down hard, and continued to wail from the floor.

"I'll show you! I'll do it the right way, you wait and see!"

— 4 —

The luxuriant growth of flowers thronging both sides of the road seemed to have floated up as one, bathing in the sun.

"It's as beautiful as they say," said Samielle PKA Freyn as the car left the starport. "And the fragrances are wonderful. Even for a while, I'd like to live on this world."

"…"

Kazeta glanced at Samielle's profile. When he first got off at the starport, Kazeta thought he hadn't changed a bit from the old days, but seen from this close, the once-stern face had softened, and his hair had thinned. He'd gotten at least that old. Maybe Kazeta looked the same in Samielle's eyes.

Even so, I wonder what Samielle meant by that, thought Kazeta. He must have heard about what happened on Tayuneine, and to Administrators who came here.

Cynicism?

Samielle wasn't the type of man to speak cynically.

"Compared to when you were an Administrator, how is it now?" he asked.

"…Mmm." Samielle left his answer at that, and without even trying to add anything, counter-questioned Kazeta.

"Cadet Thomas PPKA Jackson should be here just now, right?"

"Mmm. He's here."

Kazeta had left him in the Administration Complex.

"Something about Thomas?"

"No, no nothing."

Samielle shook his head once, and turned his eyes out the window again. The car kept moving.

"I read your situation report on Tayuneine just before I came in," said Samielle. "Is it still the same now?"

"It's gotten worse," answered Kazeta bluntly.

"Tell me about it."

Kazeta summarized the current situation, explaining it.

"So I'm part of the cause of the trouble," said Samielle as if it were humorous. "I guess I can't make a public inspection, then."

He's changed, thought Kazeta. The huge anger he used to have has vanished. Kazeta thought he liked the new Samielle better.

Suddenly SQ2A, sitting next to Kazeta, began to speak.

"SQ1 wishes to communicate with the Administrator."

"Connect us."

SQ1 began to speak through SQ2A's contact.

"The unassigned Administrator has commanded SQ2D and its group to make preparations to go out. It is not listed on his schedule, so I am reporting it to you."

"Go out? Where to?"

"SQ2D has received an order to go to the ruins where the greatest number of colonists have gathered. According to LQ1, the site corresponding to that command at this time is east-northeast of the Administration Complex, at a distance of about forty kilometers."

Kazeta knew the spot, as it was the location of the largest ruins.

"Will you issue a cancellation order?" asked SQ1.

"No, let him go," directed Kazeta. He wanted to see what Thomas would do. Then he ordered SQ2A to direct the car to those ruins.

Overgrown with trees and flowers, huge slabs of stone, step-like, were scattered in a complex arrangement across the huge caldera-shaped space, bathed in an eerie light.

The ruins.

It was still a mystery what those huge stones had been used for, what kinds of buildings had been erected on top of them. The silent existence of those scattered monoliths seemed to be smiling, sneering, at the humans trying to fathom the civilization of the native inhabitants.

But it was different now than it had always been. People were swarming over every inch of the ruins, kneeling, stretching out their arms and crying plaintively. It was a massive hymn, and had the cadence, the modulation, of countless voices.

Without any warning, a single man burst forth onto the highest slab, standing tall and upright.

"Over there! That's him, isn't it?"

By the time Samielle had spoken, Kazeta had already ordered the car to hover, and close with the man.

It was, of course, Thomas.

"Listen to me!" shouted Thomas through a hand-speaker. "Listen to me, all of you!"

The surrounding people, surprised at the noise, turned to face him.

"What you are doing is meaningless!"

Thomas' voice reached to the farthest depths of the ruins.

"No matter what you ask for, these ruins will change nothing! There are no such things as ghosts! They are nothing but illusions bred in your own minds! Do you hear me? There are no ghosts! The natives are extinct! And the dead have no power!"

Thomas bent over, picked something up, and waved it.

It was a nerve-tissue destructor.

"Go home!" he screamed. "Leave, go home, think it over again! There are no ghosts! Nothing can be achieved by your coming here! Go! Go! I'll kill you if you don't go!"

Kazeta understood.

Thomas was trying to move the people of Tayuneine with a speech and a gun. He held to his theory, and was going to prove it to them.

Terrified people beseeching the spirits for help weren't going to be moved by that.

Thomas might even murder them, if things went badly. Their hatred would focus on Thomas, then.

Dangerous.

Kazeta's car had already landed next to SQ2D's car, at the base of the stone.

"Stop!" thundered Kazeta, bursting out of the car.

"Get out of my way!"

Thomas turned the handgun towards Kazeta.

"Mind your own business, failure!"

"Stop, Thomas."

"Shut up!" shouted Thomas. "It's lazy bastards like you that are guiding these idiots! You value this warm lazy life more than the Federation!"

The people gathered across the ruins silently watched the spectacle.

"Thomas, come down. This is the Inspector!"

Just as Samielle's voice rang out, it happened. The people screamed. Mixed in with their voices, Thomas' could be heard.

"What the…! This is impossible…! No! Impossible!"

At the same time, Kazeta felt the warm presence he was used to.

The shadows.

The pale green shadows, hundreds of them, were swarming through the ruins. The shadows so sweet and warm to him were terrifying the people, making them flatten themselves to the ground, or flee screaming in sheer terror.

And Thomas.

They were pure terror to Thomas, too.

He had dropped his speaker and gun, and stood with both arms hanging limply, screaming.

"No! No! I can't be seeing… Stop it! Don't come any closer!"

Kazeta clearly saw a large group of shadows floating towards Thomas, clustering towards the top of that slab.

"Help! Stop! Go away!"

Thomas hid his face behind his hands, and tottered a few steps back. He lost his balance, and fell tumbling down.

At once, SQ2D and its retinue shifted to where he lay.

Kazeta and Samielle ran over, too.

"Is he all right?"

When Kazeta asked, the answer came slowly from SQ2D, which was already suffering functional damage due to its inability to protect Thomas.

"Life processes are… not stopped… Recovery possible… I… judged… no danger… to the unassigned… Administrator's life… and caused… this accident…"

"Take him to the Administration Complex at once and treat him," order Kazeta to SQ2A, and then noticed the atmosphere was strange, and looked up.

What...?

He looked up at the slab where Thomas had been standing.

The shadows were still clustered there. As they clustered, they came drifting slowly down towards him... But there was no longer any terror on the faces of the people that saw them.

"Look!" someone shouted. "That's not the shape of the natives! It's pale green! It's just a pale green blur!"

"What is it?" asked a different man. "Just by looking at it, I feel so good inside..."

"Aren't they... The spirits of the natives?"

"The spirits of the natives punished that evil man!"

"That's true! They took the shapes they did to make us reflect! When we showed them the proper respect again, they revealed themselves to us!"

"I feel so warm, so happy!"

They were right.

What they were seeing now was what he had seen all along. Somehow, he sensed it directly.

The shadows came down around him, and then finally vanished.

I was blessed, he thought... Or maybe it was just a whim, a caprice of the shadows... In any case, it took much longer than usual for the warmth in his heart to fade.

But... Why?

What was this phenomenon, really? What were those shadows? Were they really the spirits of the native inhabitants? That was impossible. Impossible, but... What were they? Maybe the final form of the vanished native inhabitants – or maybe they were another life-form that humanity didn't know, and had no connection at all with the vanished race.

He didn't know.

Still, wasn't it acceptable for there to be something he didn't know? To have something inexplicable by human knowledge...

"Kazeta."

Samielle clapped him on the shoulder.

"Kazeta. What are you mooning about?"

"Ah…"

He returned to himself. When he looked around, he saw that all of the people had vanished from the ruins.

"I didn't see anything," said Samielle as they were returning. "I just can't believe it's the supernatural force you say it is. I can explain it even with Thomas' hypothesis."

"How? Through a simple psychological trick?"

"No, not just that."

Samielle pursed his lips.

"Another cause can be imagined. For example, this atmosphere."

"The atmosphere?"

"Right. This air is always full of a variety of smells. Wouldn't it be effectively impossible to detect some gas or pollen that caused people to see illusions? If you consider that it only takes effect after some time, then it makes sense. People are, after all, always afraid of something, always looking over their shoulders. That fear just appeared as those ghosts, that's all."

"…"

Now that he thought about it, it seemed possible… Which meant that he had the type of mind that could give birth to that warm shadow. That he had birthed that warmth, that kindness, from the start.

He didn't know. He decided to think about it at length, later.

"I would like to caution you about Thomas PPKA Jackson," said Samielle. "You've no doubt already figured it out by now, but he's not a real cadet."

"Not real… ? But his qualifications were…"

"He's qualified. But he's only a quick-assembly unassigned Administrator, taking this course for appearances' sake. He won't become a real Administrator."

"What do you mean?"

"He's targeted to become an Inspector."

"…"

Kazeta looked at him suspiciously.

"The Federation initiated the Inspector program to monitor the Administrators," continued Samielle. "They can't, of course, make somebody Inspector who's never had experience as Administrator, so they had to take somebody from the ranks of we Administrators. Still, no matter how much they train us and retrain us, we're still both Administrators – the Inspectors and the inspected – it's only a natural development. True Administrators have always loved their worlds more than they've loved the Federation – and we're even proud of it. That's why the Federation decided to try raising an Inspector from the very beginning."

"From the start?"

"Right. They decided to make a loyal watchdog for the Federation, with only the vaguest Administration experience. Accelerated education, field training reduced to the minimum, and even then run him around worlds where everything is going well. The problem is that the number of worlds where everything is going well is limited, as there are so many where second- and third-generation colonists are having problems with their Administrators. So, just as I suspect you noticed, he was assigned to peaceful Tayuneine, where it is obviously impossible to gain any real field experience."

"…"

When he considered it now, all of Thomas' utterances fit perfectly.

"Well, it'll be different when they do their own inspecting… You're here now, so relax and be merry."

Samielle continued, "Before, I talked about my own beliefs concerning the spirits, but the fact is that as an Inspector it doesn't make any difference. I came up from being an Administrator, and don't really care if they are real ghosts or just runaway psychological problems… Just as long as the government runs smoothly."

"…"

"But it's going to be tough from now on. I think now that they've lost their fear, and have begun to beg the spirits for protection instead, that now those same spirits are going to become the targets of a type of religious fervor... And you're going to be forced into the role of standing between the gods and the believers... It's going to be tough."

Kazeta nodded.

Outside the car was a solid stretch of flower-covered prairie... The sweet fragrances flowed in through the open window. They'd arrive at the Administration Complex soon.

Tayuneine.

It wasn't bad.

And in time... Or rather, at the appointed time, he'd meet Raine again.

At that special tiny ruin.

Bound Janus

— I —

Maybe it was better to call it a shaft, a mine shaft, rather than a tunnel. The greed for that damp glistening, which could only be found by burrowing into the mountain, was obvious from that incline... As always, be they mountains of metal, or silicate, or diamond. As he trod along the center of the tunnel, heavy cold air crawled up his legs, embraced him as if to call forth ancestral memories. That wind issued from the unknown mysteries deep in the gloom of the tunnel.

Ahead of Sei PPKC Konda and SQ2A in the procession were Gun'gazea holding high an edge-lit metal candle holder, and the four Gun'gazea that had become D'o. Behind Sei came another dozen or so Gun'gazea, but all of them shuffled forward, as if checking each gloom-enwrapped step. In spite of it, their footsteps melded together, echoing into an unexpectedly loud reverberation.

The timber and cement reinforced walls of the tunnel gave way to natural rock in less than twenty meters. It was obvious from the reflections of the dim candles that the walls were dripping with water, even without touching them.

The Gun'gazea were all silent. Sei, who had been to a Gun'gazea Vault of the Dead many times, kept trudging along in respectful silence, through the twisting, winding descent he knew would become a clawing ascent on the return.

Suddenly the candles that had been lighting the walls lost their support, became solitary. They had come to the main chamber.

In a few seconds, his eyes adjusted, and he could dimly make out the high rock ceiling and the line of fourteen or fifteen statues clustered together up ahead.

This was the Vault of the Dead. It was standard, even the scale of it. The Gun'gazea stopped, and knelt down before the group of statues.

Sei followed suit.

The Gun'gazea that was the oldest D'o signaled the other three D'o to advance forward with it to the statues.

The silence shattered under its own weight, and became a low murmur. The sacred incantation, the hymn, had started.

The oldest D'o placed its hand on the shoulder of the youngest, just recently become a D'o, and raised its voice higher. After this rite, it would be formally recognized within the tribe as a D'o. In other words, a physiological D'o would now become a social D'o.

Still kneeling, Sei watched the backs of the four D'o. Judging from the color and cut of their gowns, three were female and one was male, but their hardened skin, turned greenish-black, showed clearly that distinctions of sex no longer had any meaning. While they were still Gun'gazea, they were now D'o, and nothing but D'o.

Strange, thought Sei. The D'o were unmistakably the nobility of the Gun'gazea. But was there any social structure in existence except the Gun'gazea that demanded, as a condition for becoming noble, the onset of a hardening disease that promised death in a few years? Of course, it was possible to find parallels in the ancient Terran tales of sacred kings and immortal hermits, but the sacred kings were merely living sacrifices for the ceremonies, and the hermits were obviously quite separate from the power elite. They weren't a systematized, ranked ruling class like the Gun'gazea D'o.

The basic reason it all developed was that this world, Gun'gazen, was far too rich in metals. The crust of Gun'gazen contained an immense amount of metallic elements, either as ores or ionic compounds, and the native organisms had some very special characteristics as a result of the complex interactions these metals had with their life chemistry.

Prominent among them was the hardening of the skin.

A great many of the lower life forms of Gun'gazen protected themselves with a unique skin made up of multiple layers of chitin and metal. The hardening that inevitably came to the skin was in some respect common to the life cycle of all fauna on Gun'gazen. Among the slightly more advanced animals, when the skin hardened after a soft-skinned period, it would be shed, to be followed by another period of soft skin, in a recurring cycle. The soft-skinned period of the even higher animals was much longer, and they could avoid the problem a number of times by shedding their skins, but their lifetimes were limited. If they failed to shed their skins, they became hard dead statues in the shape of their living forms.

Sei knew that those death-statues, especially that of the small creature called a "devilcat", were valued as works of art among the colonists here on Gun'gazen. The statues of the devilcat (or in the Gun'gazea language, *tsuẓuluru*) were being traded at high prices thanks to the iridescent colors of the skin, and its facial expression, which looked as if the beast were holding all the worries of the world on its shoulders. The older and bigger the statue was, the happier the colonists. It would be totally irrelevant to complain about treating a corpse like a work of art. In human eyes, the devilcat statue was certainly beautiful, and the Gun'gazea themselves worshipped the metallic corpses of their leaders, the D'o. The corpse assumed its own special existence, here. Human scientists had studied the life forms of Gun'gazen, with their special activity during the hard-skinned periods, and their deaths enwrapped in what had been their armor. They reported that there seemed to be a natural mechanism operating here such that when the organism became unable to excrete the necessary amount of metals, the skin hardened, leading to a much higher internal metabolic level.

At any rate, it was a fact that the underlying drive of evolution on Gun'gazen was escape from the metallic restrictions of the environment. At the leading edge of that evolutionary flow stood the Gun'gazea, the highest form of life on the world, who so closely resembled humanity. They had evolved to the point where they didn't shed their skins at all, but rather, after twenty or thirty years, (a Gun'gazen year corresponded to about two Terran years), they entered the first period of hardening, which promised death to come.

Considered from an evolutionary viewpoint, this hardening of the Gun'gazea illustrated the abhorrent truth that they had not yet totally escaped the curse that ruled their world. To shatter that curse, it would be necessary to lead a life without that hardening of the skin... Or at least, from the Terran point of view. Among the Gun'gazea there were a few (a very few) seriously researching exactly that point. They were striving to liberate the Gun'gazea from the fate of other Gun'gazen organisms.

Still, those Gun'gazea were looked down upon as heretics. According to the general belief of the Gun'gazea, what they were trying to do was unacceptable. To the majority of the Gun'gazea, they couldn't lose the chance of becoming D'o, even if it did mean death. As was seen in other organisms, the Gun'gazea who entered the period of hardening also became suddenly active metabolically. In particular, their ability to think and make decisions sharpened, and they wanted to exercise their minds. In addition, as the hardening of their skins made them able to withstand a high degree of damage from clubs and swords, they were the strongest warriors, and, to the Gun'gazea, led a valuable existence. In short, the D'o were perceived as a higher organism than the average Gun'gazea.

And not only that.

Among the Gun'gazea, there was also a feeling of the natural cycle of things. They felt that the common destiny they shared with all life on Gun'gazen – of hardening leading to death – was natural, and that the cycle of Gun'gazea to D'o to statue was the correct way, was the confirmation of the providence of nature.

To the Gun'gazea, escaping death by accident or disease (and these were very common ends) and living long enough to become a D'o meant that the individual was "selected," and until death came in the form of their final hardening they had the right and responsibility to utilize their capabilities for the group. The Gun'gazea were perhaps insensitive to death, or at least looked at it as an honorable and fitting end to a life, and nothing to fear. The responsibilities and rights of the D'o were significantly greater than those of most Gun'gazea, and so they earned their respect. While suffering under an enormously heavily body weight they performed tasks far beyond those of their younger brethren, and those who excelled were honored with a place in the Vault of the Dead.

The difference between the ordinary D'o and those that were twice-selected, that were finally emplaced in the Vault of the Dead, was clear from looking at even a single example. A D'o might be killed – "sent to eternal repose" was the more accurate translation – but once they were enshrined, they would not be touched even if their nation ceased to exist. Just as the living D'o were sacred and inviolate to their own tribe, so were the enshrined inviolate to all D'o as a group. It was the custom that when one nation eliminated another, the conquering side assumed the duty of protecting the Vault of the Dead in place of the vanished ones.

The chant was still continuing.

Sei lifted his eyes slowly and looked at the group of statues lined up ahead of him. They had led their nation through decisive battles that had determined its existence, or perhaps invented a new technology to save them all from famine. They had now become statues, as they were when alive, and waited for their ranks to swell.

No.

They looked just as they had during their lives, but all that remained now was the exterior. The older ones should be totally lacking their insides. Their hollow metal shells preserved the shapes of their corpses...

Sei suddenly, for no apparent reason, recalled the Administrator System, of which he himself was a member. The memory almost forced itself upon him... The Administrator System that had, over the seventy years since its inception, been rebuilt and reorganized in response to changing conditions and the passage of time, achieving many of its goals while having many of its contradictions exposed. The system that the Federation had built up, employing the finest brains to firm up its foundation, and driven by the greatest authority... As a system, it was unquestionably superior, and somehow amazingly durable.

But it was not perfect... It couldn't be. Wasn't this system, with problems cropping up continuously both on colonial worlds and in the Central Body itself, already like those corpses, nothing but a giant exoskeleton with the vital interior rotted away?

Sei brought has gaze back into focus.

The chant was finally ending, and the rite was entering the final stage.

The newly-created D'o made a final obeisance to the statues, then turned his way. Sei hadn't noticed, but a pottery jar with the national mark set in it had already been laid on the floor in front of it. It was a simple, lightly-glazed jar.

The Gun'gazea raised their voices into a roar together, their tails stretching out across the floor. Just as it peaked, changing voices suddenly to a strange harmony, the new D'o raised its arms, and smashed the jar with the sword it held. The Gun'gazea shouted excitedly to each other, praising the superb body of the new D'o. By passing through this ancient ritual, the new D'o was accepted into the ranks of the D'o through social acclaim.

When all was finished, silence descended again. The Gun'gazea began to rise silently and return to the surface. Sei and SQ2A maintained their places in the line.

That shuffling progress started again.

When Sei thought about his own position in the rite, he sometimes felt the humor of it, as if he were adrift in space. All of the Gun'gazea, of whatever nation, had strict rules defining who was allowed to participate in the ceremony. Among them, the position that the Administrator held was exceedingly strange and ill-defined. He was not a guiding member of the nation, but neither was he a visitor from another nation, or a mediator. He had been allowed to participate with his status remaining ill-defined. Naturally, Gun'gazea who were picky about formalities had made "Administrator" a special qualification, and thus invited him. They were recognizing the decades of effort that the Administrators had put in, using their robots, to introduce new technology and to foster better relations between nations. While the Gun'gazea understood he had a responsibility to protect the interests of the colonists who had come to this world, they also recognized that the Administrator, who brought new tools and methods over the years, had become necessary to their own lives. His special need to help both sides, the colonists and the native inhabitants, progress simultaneously, like a two-faced god, had made itself visible in this vague special status accorded him.

The Administrator was sometimes treated as the eldest D'o, occasionally as a mere rankless outsider. Once in a while he was received as an enemy. His status changed in response to the attitude of that particular nation and their personal reactions. Sei rapidly learned how to respond flexibly, as had the previous Administrator, as befit his unstable position. He had become supple, but that wasn't to say he enjoyed this temporary stability followed by a sudden shift of status. That would be impossible. All he could do was to make a habit of constant reflection on his best course of action. From that viewpoint, the fact that he had been present at the ceremony from start to finish was due to one of two things: either he was being genuinely received as a friend, or they wished to use his driving power for something.

They left the tunnel, and the heat returned.

It wasn't easy to press through the luxuriant trees along that narrow path. The unworked ground was rough, and he felt he would stumble if he relaxed his attention even for a moment. The sunlight here was only a trickle that dripped down through the overhanging leaves, but even so it was hot enough to feel on his skin.

He kept walking. There was no other choice. Overhead flew a number of LQQ-class robots monitoring the vicinity, and his personal craft, that had waited outside the cave, followed him now at the end of the procession. It would be so easy simply to ride, but of course he couldn't. When walking with the Gun'gazea, you had to use your own feet if you wished to be treated properly by them. The Gun'gazea looked with distaste upon those who made more tools than were needed, or who used them when unnecessary. In particular, to use a vehicle to attend today's ceremony would be nothing if not rude.

After about twenty minutes of walking through the forest, at last the low wall of the fortification appeared – it was made of cast iron poles, the cracks filled in with clay, and overlaid with a coating of mortar. The section facing the road was a gate.

The procession passed through that gate, and continued on inside. Inside the gate was a glittering plaza. The hardened skin of the four D'o, like finely woven fabric, caught the rays of the sun and shone an iridescent greenish-black. Their skins exhibited considerable differences depending on the district; some were glistening black, and others bright gold or blue. Perhaps it was due to the different concentrations of metallic salts left in their bodies, but in all cases it still caused the same hardening, the same angularity, the same brocade-like iridescent skin.

As there were D'o in the procession, the dozens of Gun'gazea working and talking in the plaza stopped, faced the line, and bowed, lowering their heads in respect.

Surrounding the plaza were dozens of large buildings. Most of them were two-story, but a few were three stories tall. They used many and various metals, finishing off the detail in wood... To human eyes they were just the frames of buildings, although they had windows, too. The buildings were much wider than they were tall, and the windows were real glass, however poor the quality. Their transparency was none too good, and they were bluish, so they were primarily used for lighting, rather than for seeing in or out.

Of all those buildings, only one – symmetrical, with three storeys – was built of steel and aluminum alloy. It was the newest building, erected with the help of the robots using the highest precision materials the robots made. Behind the main buildings were lines of barracks for the middle- and low-class members, then the agricultural and livestock areas, the industrial area with the coke ovens and the kilns, and finally the military training ground – but of course most of it was hidden from the plaza.

There were many different varieties of clothing and objects, reflecting the fact that this city was made up of many different groups, each distinct from the others. Still, there was the sense of a strictly-maintained, intricate, yet invisible thread binding them together. Scattered across the face of Babel continent were over two hundred nations of roughly the same character, in competition. The larger ones had populations of one hundred forty or one hundred fifty thousand, and the smaller ones seven or eight thousand, but none were any larger or smaller than those limits.

There was a reason for this.

In the larger nations, as the population grew too big, so did the number of D'o, and government functions became paralyzed. Most of the Gun'gazea died before the skin-hardening began. Not only in combat and from disease, but also their primitive mining techniques were extremely dangerous, with high fatality rates. As a result, only a very few were able to become D'o: usually about one D'o for every six to eight thousand population... The nations of one hundred fifty thousand had about twenty D'o, which meant that it was difficult to reach consensus during policy decisions. Even though the Gun'gazea society used group leadership, that was only practicable when the number of leaders was, at the most, seven or eight . Whereas humans would commonly create a smaller council at the top, or form a core group, the Gun'gazea hadn't developed that way. It was the feeling of the Gun'gazea that while there were differences between the ages of the D'o, there should be no orders given or received among them. Regardless of how young a D'o might be, a D'o was still a D'o. The only method left to them was for the smaller faction to withdraw, and begin a new nation with their following of Gun'gazea. This gave the appearance that the Gun'gazea enjoyed a level autonomy that allowed withdrawal from the group based on individual judgment, but this was not the case. It was merely that the Gun'gazea were proud of the D'o that came from their own tribe, and followed them. In other words, when the number of D'o, the only nobility in Gun'gazea society, increased beyond a certain number, the nation automatically divided. The upper limit seemed to be about twenty D'o, as there were no nations with more than that number.

In the same way, there was a lower limit on the size of smaller nations. A group without any D'o was not socially recognized as a nation. For that reason, the smallest nations had to be composed of a group with at least a single D'o. It was theoretically possible for a single D'o to rule over a group of two or three thousand Gun'gazea, but in fact there were no tribes of less than seven or eight thousand, as it was difficult to become economically independent without a minimum number of workers in each field... It was wiser to join a larger nation, and wait for their numbers to grow. In that case, it also happened that additional D'o came out of the tribe, creating a power structure within the nation, and giving the tribe greater influence over the entire nation.

This reflected the complicated interactions of the Gun'gazea. It was true that the D'o were, in a sense, representatives acting for the benefit of their own tribes, but that attitude was harshly criticized. It was natural for the tribe to be proud of the D'o they produced, but also for the D'o to dedicate themselves to the entire nation, not just their tribe. It showed the special elite sensitivity of the D'o themselves, having left their tribes and submerged themselves into the vague, sexless, levelless D'o.

In this sense, the nation that Sei was visiting now, Kuwast, was an example of a nation keeping its balance well. It had started as a splinter group thirty years before, developed smoothly, and had now reached the level of eight D'o and almost seventy thousand Gun'gazea. It was a group that hadn't forgotten its origins, and still had goals for the future.

The procession and its dark shadows cut across the plaza and entered the new building, which was being used as the government center of the nation.

One of the Gun'gazea who had come to greet them led Sei and SQ2A to a separate room, and asked them to wait for a while.

Sei sat down in one of the chairs facing the table, and told SQ2A to stand behind him. He sighed lightly.

It was hot.

The temperature was unquestionably over forty Celsius, but since the building was built for Gun'gazea there was, of course, no air conditioning.

Sei glanced over the maps pasted on the wall. They were all maps that had been surveyed and drawn by the robots. The Administration Complex of Gun'gazen, which had originally made the maps for the human settlers, had made them available to anyone who asked about twenty years ago. The demand had been growing with every year, and now they charged a small fee – and expenses – making it a kind of sales operation. It was also true that a variety of problems had come up since the Administration Complex had begun to charge for services that had once been free, and not only for the maps. There were about ten modes of payment, ranging from the coins he had minted, through the various currencies used by the colonial governments, to the gold, silver, alloys, mercury or rough gems of the Gun'gazea... And the problem was how to set the relative prices... Or to slide with the market. Recently, the demand from the Gun'gazea had become remarkably high. Now, the average nation had at least five or six sets of maps.

The map on the far right-hand side of the wall was the world map of Gun'gazen. In the center was the rather mundane shape of the continental group, and Unity Island where the Administration Complex was located. Naturally, the Administrator at the time had drawn the map such that the "Greenwich line" of this world ran through the center of the Administration Complex.

The name Unity Island had no particular meaning, and had been chosen by the first military governor assigned here. Maybe he'd wanted to raise morale, or improve his standing with his superiors. As proof that he hadn't been merely a duty-bound drudge with no personal feelings at all, the island just south of Unity Island was called Hawke Island, after himself.

North of Unity Island spread the "island group", with nine major islands and over a hundred smaller ones. The arrangement of the nine islands suggested the rough profiles of a beak, or a wing, or legs or tail, and together gave the impression of some strange bird. It had been given the name Rhamphorynchus Archipelago, after the flying reptile of the Terran Jurassic Period. That being somewhat hard to pronounce in everyday conversation, it was generally called "The Archipelago".

Perhaps because the Rhamphorynchus Archipelago was so far north, it hadn't been colonized by the Gun'gazea yet, so the human settlers moved in. Almost ten million settlers had formed nine governments centered on the nine islands, built their cities, and were progressing with industrial development. Perhaps not quite nine *separate* governments... Although the Administrator hadn't officially recognized it yet, they were moving towards government through a single large organization.

Between Unity Island and the Archipelago was the Resort Group, famous for its clear, alluring sun and sea, and beyond that, to the east, south, and west, spread the Fishing Islands. Farther to the west, beyond the Fishing Islands – due south of Unity Island and Hawke Island – were the Jellyfish Islands. They had some limited tourist and fishing spots, but hadn't been developed yet by either humans or Gun'gazea.

There was also the silent continent – the polar continent. It was a totally undeveloped, wild land spreading across the north pole, uninhabited except for a robot observation center monitoring the movements of its animals.

And then there was Babel.

The continent of Babel, which extended from the southwest of Unity Island, was the largest land body on this world of sea and sail, and it was the world of the Gun'gazea.

It looked like… No, it would be best to look at the map of Babel pasted on the wall. Babel presented an indistinct shape, like a potato, with one major mountain range. This range included the tallest mountain on Gun'gazen, Babel – that was what the Gun'gazea themselves called it, and as its shape reminded the humans of the Tower of Babel, the name had been adopted directly from the Gun'gazea tongue. There was a jungle belt in the southeast with three major rivers, and north of that stretched the huge Babel desert.

The third map was of the northern part of the jungle, where the Kuwast lived. Areas that had been unsurveyed, or had changed, had been corrected here and there by the Gun'gazea, including the names and locations of new nations. These maps were updated every ten years, and the robots were surveying even now… Maybe ten years was just too long, thought Sei.

If there was enough time to do it…

Maybe there wasn't time anymore.

Sei turned.

With heavy footsteps on the metal floor, four D'o came in. From their clothing, Sei could tell that two of them had attended the rite, even though otherwise they all looked the same. One of those two was the eldest D'o, and the other was today's newly recognized D'o. The others, who had not taken part in the rite, were no doubt handling the day-to-day affairs of the community.

The four D'o sat down slowly directly across from Sei, but said nothing.

Following them, seven or eight Gun'gazea came in, and stood behind the D'o, making preparations to record the meeting. They weren't D'o, but were doubtless the highest-status veteran officials, acting here only as scribes and bodyguards.

After preparations were finished, one of the D'o spoke, for the first time. It was one of the two that had not taken part in the rite, and, as he remembered, had been second or third to gain D'o status in Kuwast. When the Gun'gazea spoke their nostrils flared, and their peculiar fast speech reflected the fact that they were barely breathing. Since he had come here, over a year ago – or two, by Terran standards – Sei had come to be able to use Gun'gazea speech, but it was still totally impossible to understand or speak at the speed the D'o used.

"We apologize for making you wait," translated SQ2A, and Sei nodded in return.

"Thank you for granting us your precious time during your regular inspection rounds," continued the D'o. "As the representatives of Kuwast we are in the position of having to make a request of you as the controller of the robots, possessed of the highest power and technology."

"What would that be?" asked Sei in his own language, and SQ2A translated.

"Your predecessor, and you yourself, have forbidden trade between the Gun'gazea, including we Kuwast, and the colonist nations living in the cold lands to the north. This edict is still in effect, is it not?"

"It is."

What the D'o had said was true, but Sei wanted to prevent a one-sided interpretation. "However, this policy is only until the worlds of the Gun'gazea and that of the humans can interact without great loss or friction. In other words, it is an edict that will be repealed at some future point.

"At the present time, though, it is still in force."

"That is correct."

"Even so, illicit trading has been going on under your predecessor and under yourself, and the scale has been increasing with each year. Are you aware of this?"

Of course he knew, and it was exactly for that reason that he was building a public trading center on the southern tip of Unity Island. Things had progressed to that point. Along with the human expansion had come the smuggling, finally becoming glaringly obvious about ten years ago, and growing worse every year. No matter how many times he exposed it, he couldn't destroy its roots. The robots had sunken ships and arrested smugglers, but the situation had gotten even worse these last few months. Maybe they were enthralled by the vast profit attainable, but recently some colonists were willing to resist to the death.

Not only that.

According to the robots stationed in the Archipelago, a number of colonists had been killed during the arrests, and the facts of the story had been twisted in the telling to make it look like murder. This gave rise to a very strong enmity towards the robots among the colonists. On the one hand, he had ordered SQ1 (*That damned* SQ1...) to use its judgment and act to extinguish that enmity, while on the other he had started construction of an official trade center where he could check and control all trade. This would at least be better than the present situation.

The opening of the trade center was being put off until the colonists and the Gun'gazea both began to raise a demand for it. For the moment, he would hold it in abeyance, keeping track of the smuggling situation, and wait for the perfect timing.

For which reason, of course, he couldn't talk about it with the D'o seated across from him now.

"I am aware of the illicit trading," he nodded. "And, as you know, we continue our patrols, and punish both colonists and Gun'gazea alike as we find them."

A metallic crash rang out.

The eldest D'o, seated to the right, had dropped its arm to the table. Sei wasn't sure if it was accidental, or if it held some sort of threat, of warning.

"That also is so," rumbled the eldest D'o deeply. "You and your robots are always impartial. Leaving aside for the moment the point of whether that is actually possible or not, you attempt to be so. But isn't the age of that policy's effectiveness now over?"

"..." By the time Sei had shifted his attention, the D'o was relaxed in its chair again, and talking in a humor-filled voice.

"Excuse me, excuse me. I didn't mean to be rude; I was merely expressing my feelings."

Sei bowed. What else could he do? What else could he do when faced with a fact that he himself had already accepted?

It was hot.

In contrast to the glittering outside views, the room was dark, but now that very darkness seemed to be making it hotter. And he wasn't sure if the droplets of sweat rolling down his back were only due to the heat... He kept his face expressionless as he wondered.

"At any rate, the illicit trading is continuing as before despite your efforts," continued the first D'o. "A number of nations near us are violating this edict."

"How do you know this?"

"Because those nations – the very strong Toka and Cotoru among them – have made extremely heavy demands of us. They have raised the prices of the goods we purchase from them, and have insisted that we pay either in the currency issued by the Administrator, or in devilcats... if we refuse them directly, it seems it will unavoidably lead to war."

The D'o took a breath, and continued.

"We Kuwast are not the biggest of tribes, but we have more than enough force to protect ourselves, and they know that. In spite of that fact, they are willing to fight us, which can only mean that they have received weapons from the colonists that we do not possess, and therefore have confidence in their ability to win."

"At the present time, there are twenty-one D'o in the Toka, and nineteen in the Cotoru. They have made preparations for war," added the youngest D'o.

Sei nodded

It was all just as they said.

What would happen to a tribe when it had more than the necessary number of D'o, but had neither reached the point where governmental functions became paralyzed, nor birthed splinter groups? Or, what would happen as the rights of each individual D'o became smaller and smaller while functioning within the nation? Recalling that there were no distinctions of higher or lower, better or worse, among the D'o. Human common sense suggested a change from government by council to government by a noble class, growing rapidly in size, and creating many various structures and functions. The Gun'gazea, though, didn't do that. Whether they sensed the limits of the nation, or whether their methods of government and imagination simply hadn't progressed to the point where they could handle a population of hundreds of thousands, or millions, he didn't know, but at any rate, they didn't let the population of a nation exceed one hundred forty or one hundred fifty thousand. Before that, they fought. As a result of the combat, the winning side gave eternal rest – death – to the vanquished D'o, and sent their own D'o to rule in their place.

To human eyes, that looked like conquest and provincial rule, but it was natural to the Gun'gazea. Regardless of the situation, all responsibility for the combat rested with the D'o, and it was better to give them eternal rest than to remove their authority. Even the losing side, though, needed D'o to be a nation, and so new D'o were dispatched from the winning side.

Sei could understand it thus far, but after that point it became incomprehensible to a Terran. That was because the outcome of a war varied widely depending on the combat, the relationship of the nations involved, and the mood of the moment. Sometimes a single D'o would go alone, sometimes with its group; sometimes a number of D'o would go, sometimes taking their groups. It was further complicated by the fact that sometimes intermarriage was forbidden, and at other times enforced, and there was also a wide variety of approaches to the rights of ceremony and the care of the Vault of the Dead. If you asked the Gun'gazea directly, they didn't say much about it, and even those that were willing to talk didn't know anything but their own opinions. Naturally, the robots had tried to analyze the situation under the orders of one of the previous Administrators, to see exactly what situation led to what kind of result, but they hadn't been very successful. There were so many aspects that changed with time and so many that couldn't be adequately quantified, and in spite of the need to define all these factors, the robots seemed to have nailed down so very few. They hadn't even clarified the interrelationships between all that many of them yet. *Anyway...* Perhaps in another fifty or sixty years there would be enough data to reach some sort of conclusion, but at the moment it merely served to show the wide distance between two apparently similar intelligent species.

But... All that didn't matter today.

It was clear that Kuwast was being targeted by the other nations. Both Toka and Cotoru each had a hundred and ten to a hundred and twenty thousand Gun'gazea, and about twenty D'o, and with that relatively large number of D'o, they were likely to invade another nation.

"In other words, we are being threatened by your failure to fully carry out enforcement of your edict," pointed out the fourth, hitherto silent D'o, mildly but firmly.

"... I see."

Sei had to answer something.

"Based on this situation, we, for the good of Kuwast, are left with no alternative but to make a petition to you," spoke the eldest D'o.

Sei felt the back of his combination watch/communicator begin to pulse regularly against his skin.

A signal.

It was the emergency signal that SQ1 sent through the action chief (in this case, SQ2) to alert Sei during a meeting that couldn't be interrupted.

What had happened?

Of course, Sei revealed nothing, and responded to the other.

"Petition, you said?"

"Yes, a petition," said the eldest D'o. "We of Kuwast have respected your edict up until now. As a result, we are being threatened by those who have violated it. We therefore petition you to remove the threat from Kuwast."

"What do you want me to do?"

"Either collect the weaponry that Toka and Cotoru have gained through this trade, or use your force to destroy them... But I suppose that's impossible..."

"It is. If I were to enter their land to search for those weapons, I would never find them all, and the action itself would be interpreted by you Gun'gazea as a war against your species. It is totally outside my authority as Administrator to consider destroying a nation."

As he was answering, he felt the signal again. It must be an extreme emergency, indeed.

"For those reasons, we believe you should loan us the needed weaponry to fight with and conquer Toka and Cotoru, officially."

"Weaponry?"

This is a tough one, thought Sei. One mistake would be condemned from all sides as favoritism, and if he gave weaponry to all sides to avoid favoritism, the entire world would soon be in a war stance, and the problem would escalate. It was impossible.

"We realize this is extremely difficult, " said the D'o that had spoken first. "We have expressed some specific ideas. If you reject them, then you must protect Kuwast through some other means, in the name of the Administrator and in the name of the one that forbade smuggling. You must remove by some means the threat over Kuwast... This is our petition."

"I understand your petition in full."

Sei bowed his head lightly. For this type of problem, he couldn't give a quick answer even if he was already decided. If he acquiesced easily, there would be other demands, and if he refused at once the others would be offended, and lose face. Of course, he knew all too well that this reflection was undeniably Administrator-ish, and served to entrench his own authority. For now, he had to discuss it fully with SQ1 and develop a solid platform from which to respond. He had already felt the emergency signal for the third time, and he had to find out what the problem was as soon as possible.

"We will investigate immediately as to whether we can respond to your petition or not. If we accept your proposal, we will carry it out at once. However, if there should be an alternative way to protect your safety, then I would like to discuss it further with you, either here or at the Administration Complex. Is that acceptable to you?"

"May we expect your reply soon?"

"Of course."

"In that case, it is acceptable," answered the eldest D'o, after exchanging glances with the other three.

"May I interpret this to mean that our conversation is finished for the time being?"

"..."

The four D'o silently lowered their heads.

"In that case, excuse me. I thank you sincerely for the privilege and honor of being allowed to attend your rite today. It was glorious."

Sei finished his leave-taking formally, and stood up.

As he did, the heat came burning back. He could hear the sound of metal being forged somewhere.

— 2 —

The Administrator's craft and the LQQ-class robots which had been inconspicuously protecting him had already taken up formation for the return flight.

As soon as he entered the craft, his breathing grew easier, and a cool breeze enwrapped his body. He sat down, opened the lock on the communicator, and spoke to SQ2A at his side.

"What happened?"

"According to the communication from SQ1, the colonists are assembling a major fleet in the southern bay of Hawke Island," reported SQ2A. "Judging from the past actions of the colonists, SQ1 believes it to be for the purpose of illicit trade."

"Not again."

"The fleet is composed of fifty ships, starting from the four thousand ton class," continued SQ2A unemotionally. "In addition, the ships are armed with advanced weaponry, including lasers. The larger vessels have magnetic resonators mounted."

"Magnetic resonators?"

As he felt the craft rise, his eyes narrowed. This wasn't the first time they had carried weaponry. It was common for them to carry arms, claiming that they were for protection from other governments or military craft. Were he to investigate it thoroughly, they would probably turn out to be in violation of the law, but as Administrator he took their psychology into account and silently accepted that much. It was hardly reasonable, though, to carry magnetic resonators. No doubt they had many excuses ready if he asked for them, but Sei had no choice but to believe they were aimed at the robots, and that they were installed for real combat against the robots.

A fifty ship fleet?

"And?" pressed Sei.

"Please hold. SQ1 wishes to communicate with you directly."

SQ2A fell silent for a moment, and then began to speak in a slightly different voice. It was, of course, SQ1 talking through SQ2A's enunciator. Due to the relatively poor quality of the speech synthesizer, it was much rougher than the voice SQ1 had in the Administration Complex.

"Reporting," said SQ1. "The fleet gathered in the southern bay of Hawke Island has begun to move south from the Rhamphorynchus Archipelago in groups of two and three towards the Resort Islands. They appear to be engaged in fishing. There are also tourist vessels and research vessels in the group. One group has taken the route usually used for smuggling, but its size is small, so they are being allowed to pass."

"They all assembled at the same point, same time?"

"Yes. They all set out for Hawke Island this morning, and began to assemble in the southern bay," said SQ1. "I am still analyzing their intercepted communications from that time, but have not yet found anything resembling commands."

"Isn't it also possible they prearranged the rendezvous before setting out?"

"It is of course possible."

"Well, we'll find that out by asking anyone we arrest. Still... We can't arrest them just for meeting at Hawke Island."

"Just so."

"If we arrest them, it'll have to be at the actual trading spot, or when they use those magnetic resonators against the robots... Was it impossible to check if they had those resonators before this problem started?"

"It was impossible."

SQ1's voice seemed to have become a little deeper, but maybe it was just his imagination.

"It appears that they loaded the parts on piece by piece and assembled them on board the vessels."

"Which means that they have a lot of technical people on board."

"Correct."

"Did you run any data checks as to the origin of the crews?"

"I am now checking... However, there are many null areas within the cities that make it impossible to run complete investigations."

"... null areas..." muttered Sei.

Null areas.

The mere fact that they had developed was a major problem.

When the first Administrator had taken over from the military Governor some twenty-five years ago (or fifty years ago, in Terran time), the population had been only some fifty thousand humans, in the otherwise uninhabited northern areas, and the Gun'gazea on the Babel continent.

Those fifty thousand people, receiving aid from the Administration Complex, proceeded to make dwellings here and there throughout the Archipelago, then established thriving towns, and constantly pressed forward with development.

Each time the Administrator ordered the robots to protect or aid the settlers, the robots took a census of the group and stored the data, while sending the needed material or labor. On this accommodating world, the colonists used the rich metallic resources to the fullest, pushing rapidly into industrial development, and raising their living standards... As a result, Gun'gazen acquired a reputation of being a world where you could make a future for yourself, and new settlers poured in, raising the population geometrically. Even so, the robots didn't stop collecting and storing data for each and every person. It was part of their job to service the immigrants.

At the present time, with the population almost exceeding ten million, that policy had come to be hated. There was a growing current of dissatisfaction, wondering why the Administrator had to keep track of every person. Plus which, the nine separate governmental bodies were now forming a single large government, which was coming into conflict with the robots, and the robots were being excluded more and more. Especially after smugglers began to die – as a result of their own suicidal resistance – the animosity towards the robots had been increasing, and now it wasn't uncommon for ordinary procedural robots to be destroyed inside the towns. Under those circumstances, it became impossible to collect personal and demographic information... And so these unmonitored areas – null areas – had come into existence over the past six months.

The robots could not tell who was in those areas, or what they might be doing.

Maybe Sei should have sent in an investigative robot team with combat capabilities, or spy robots. He had thought of it, but given the colonists' way of thinking, he felt it would be better merely to wait a little longer.

"This is the first case of its type on this world," continued SQ1, as Sei sat silent.

"After referring to your order patterns, the directives of the Federation, analysis of similar cases, and the information in the data bank, I propose the following assumptions and counter-actions. This fleet has assembled for the purpose of smuggling, and is heading for Babel continent. They are prepared to resist the robots more than they have in the past. Across their path for Babel, I have designated a line ten kilometers from the Babel continent coast as a defensive line, and stationed two hundred seventy LQS-class robots there."

"LQS-class?"

"Yes. In the past anti-smuggling operations, it has been possible to use the LX-class robots to temporarily paralyze the humans, and control their freedom of movement, but even knowing the danger, humans have stationed themselves on the sides of the ships, and have fallen into the sea to drown. This must be avoided if possible. For this reason, I have decided that it would be better to utilize the LQS-class robots to destroy the ships' propulsion systems, making it easy to collect them later in their non-controllable state."

"… Understood."

"Do you have any other directives?"

"No. Not now."

To be honest, Sei felt a little apprehensive about SQ1's strategy. SQ1 could only make decisions based on the past actions of the colonists, and Sei worried if that would be enough to handle the present situation. But what good would it do to leak that suspicion to SQ1? He added to his previous words.

"That's sufficient. At any rate, for the moment."

"Understood. I will communicate immediately any change in the situation," said sq1, and ended the communication. After a moment, the speaker adjusted its frequency, and sq2a spoke.

"Shall we return as planned to the Administration Complex?"

"Mm..."

sq2a no doubt relayed the order, because the craft suddenly regained the speed it had lost, and began to climb.

It was beautiful weather.

The thick jungle below him began to grow sparser, signaling the approach to the desert areas. Which meant that the craft, rather than taking the southern route which passed over Hawke Island, was taking the route from the northern desert of Babel, across the straits, returning from the west to Unity Island. More than likely, sq1 had reasoned that if the smugglers near Hawke Island saw his craft, they would only become more violent, and had ordered this route.

It should take another three hours to reach the Administration Complex. He didn't need to ask how long it would take, as he had flown both ways many times.

He wondered if it was really necessary to think that deeply... Was it really a benefit to take this route – as he guessed – to avoid being seen by the smugglers? Or mightn't it even have the opposite effect?

Yes.

Lately, Sei had begun to think that the robot organization of Gun'gazen, with sq1 at the top, had begun to act a little out of step with reality. Such a thing should have been impossible from the very structure of the organization, but... He felt that way.

No, maybe it was only natural. As Administrator, he knew well that the Central Body of the Federation received his reports very cautiously, almost as if they filtered them first. To look at it from another angle, it demonstrated that the Federation had lost the spirit it had had in its youth, that it had become bureaucratized. Those obese sections, afraid of being held responsible, had stopped accepting reports in their entirety.

It was true that part of the cause lay with the Administrators. The Central Body unquestionably wanted them to be loyal officials, but a large number of Administrators doggedly stuck to the original principles of the Administrator System, working not only for the Administration but for the good of their individual worlds. Not only was that the basic idea and tradition of the Administrators, but if they didn't do so they began to question their own existence, thereby losing their ability to function on their world and finally being excluded from its society. The Central Body, though, without actual experience, couldn't understand this. Even if you assumed, for a moment, that they could intellectually understand it, they would still not be able to sympathize to the point where they would protect the Administrator.

Looking at it historically, it was unavoidable that the Inspector System should have been initiated to bridge the gulf between the center and the problem.

An Inspector should be coming to Gun'gazea in the near future, too, but the Federation had stopped issuing any advance warning, to prevent the Administrator from altering anything. Well, that didn't really matter, because the presence of an Inspector was totally irrelevant to Administrators really involved in their work. The Inspectors, too, had passed a deep-level psychological probe, and were filled with the importance of their orders. They couldn't be bought. In that sense, at least, the Central Body and its members hadn't completely rotted.

It was a big question, though, exactly how accurate their reports to the Central Body were – after only two or three weeks of inspection, to report clearly on the Administrator's misses from the Central Body's perspective. For that reason, the Federation had stopped trying to respond to the Administrators' requests for new information updates for their robots' data banks. Rather than that, it was more common for them to demand government based on the initial principles and values instilled into the robots.

Could you really expect things to go well on that basis?

Wasn't it a bit peculiar to expect the well-ordered system of the colonial era, with empty worlds able to accept any number of settlers, to still apply well to this era of worlds populated many generations ago? Wasn't it only common sense that there should be a gap, a difference?

Maybe there were people who said no. Maybe there were people who said the robots had the ability to coldly analyze and solve the current situation. It was true, though, that the data implanted into the robots when they were first established on the colony worlds was the strongest, and that all future decisions were based on and made within the framework of that basic data. Things might be different if you separated the robots from their old data base, and tried to rebuild the system... But no, if they did that, the robots might well judge that the Administrator System itself was inadequate. Basically, the fundamental contradictions contained in the robots made it necessary for the government to be an "Administrator-robot" system, and for decisions to be based on that relationship – even though relations between native inhabitants and colonists had changed dramatically over the years, and the situation of the colonists themselves had altered.

Well – it couldn't be helped.

He was an Administrator. He was the Administrator that ruled the robots, and this world... There was nothing to do but to keep trying.

In spite of the situation, he couldn't deny that the robots were working hard. There was no denying they had been given the abilities to handle any situation, and even if there should be a totally unforeseen event, as there was today, they would somehow manage to analyze it within their current data array, and deal with it. Even to the bare-faced demands and actions of the colonists these days, the robots managed to respond in their own ways.

But when the question became, "Is that enough?", Sei had to think. Wasn't there bound to be a gap, given that the robots couldn't exceed their basic data by very much? The robots were still recognizing the problem as smuggling, and had changed their response to it as it grew larger. He felt that they only thought of the recent movement of the governments into a single body – the "Independence Movement" if you cared to call it that – as a sudden development... Even though it was vastly more important than smuggling. In other words, he couldn't help but feel that their inability to fear unexpected changes in their world was a fatal weakness.

Maybe he was exaggerating.

If it is was only exaggeration, then well and good.

Even so, Sei's vague uneasiness wouldn't vanish.

For example, he thought...

For example, had SQI and its robots really calculated the effects of that man's presence in the Independence Movement? Sei had questioned SQI on that point a number of times, and always received the same answer — they had taken it into account, of course. Then SQI would always ask Sei to explain why he asked the question. Sei could explain the feelings in his heart, but... He didn't feel confident that SQI had really grasped it and incorporated that hard-to-explain apprehension into its data banks.

That man.

Mischer.

Mischer YF Gainue.

Formally, he was just a colonist. He was only one of the ten million colonists and descendants of colonists on this world. At least, that was how the robots viewed him.

Still, the facts were different.

To Administrator Sei, it was different.

To Sei, Mischer wasn't just Mischer. He was "Mischer who failed as Administrator'"

Sei had met Mischer twice.

The first time... *Hmm, yes...* When he had been here half a year... One year by Terran standards...

From the very start, that middle-aged man in the group of representatives from the Archipelago governments had caught Sei's eye.

For one reason, he was a new face.

Sei had been meeting all of the other representatives a few times every month or two since he had come here. The nine different governments would send their representatives, sometimes singly, sometimes in groups, usually carrying their various requests in their hands. The different governments had varying levels of development and scale, but they all wanted the same things – universities, rail networks, shipyards, research facilities, and expanded industrial areas.

It showed that the rash concentration of colonists was still continuing, but Sei always listened to a simple explanation, and if there were no major problems, then had the robots check the minor points and correct the plan, and granted the request. That was because under the present Federation directive, this world was Class v, Type a: he should generally approve whatever the local governments wished to do, as long as it didn't interfere with the principles of Administration. There was really no need to approve each and every thing separately. It would be enough to leave it to the colonists, and just check them from going too far, and the fact that they continued to come for permission reflected not only that it had become a custom, but also that it was much easier to get technical and economic assistance from the Administrator after receiving formal permission. Still, according to the data banks, this formality had become limited to only the major projects, and they had stopped notifying the Administrator of the small jobs they could do themselves. Twenty or thirty years ago, they had requested even the smallest thing from the Administration Complex. The colonists finished many of their own construction jobs by themselves. One could say that they were only using the Administrator and his robots. Sei, though, didn't draw attention to their selfishness; instead, he merely made as much time as possible to meet with and talk to the colonists. Sei felt it was a precious chance to build harmony with the colonial side. As a result, most of the meetings became friendly talk-fests. That was Sei's feeling at least, although he didn't really know if the colonists felt the same way.

That particular day, though, didn't have that mood. A tense air hovered somewhere. It was amazing enough that representatives from all nine governments should come together. Among that group, the only new face was that rather middle-aged man. They hadn't come with an appeal or a request, but rather with a demand.

Another thing that astonished Sei was that man's attitude.

Generally, the people who came were much more conscious than need be of the fact that they were in the presence of the Administrator. That was because there were over fifty years of tradition behind the Administrator, and the Administrator was a clear symbol of authority to his audience — even if he didn't actively project himself that way. He was a phenomenon that the colonists couldn't respond to without preconceptions. To Sei, there were always the same speech patterns among the people who met him as Administrator. Either a strange friendliness, or obsequiousness... Or sometimes they would raise their heads and thrust their words at him ferociously. This man displayed none of those reactions. He was maybe fifty, fifteen or sixteen years older than Sei, with classical features. He came in with the others, sat down with them, silently casting his gaze around and about, and did nothing to break the etiquette or formality. In his eyes, though, there was an impression that he had come to meet with an equal opponent in a strictly business discussion.

I wonder who he is, thought Sei. He wished he could have investigated him before the meeting, but there had been no information other than his name in the guest book.

Sei dropped his eyes to the name list. Skipping the names he knew, he determined that the other was the representative from Kata Island, Mischer YF Gainue. Sei verified that during the greetings.

He was sure he had heard that name before, somewhere, but couldn't recall just where.

What was much more important to Sei was the fact that this man seemed to have no connection with the so-called famous families of the colonists. It was unclear if his surname was Mischer or Gainue, but both were missing from the ranks of the famous families. It was most common on Gun'gazen, which had such a long history of use as a colonial planet, for representatives to be either members of one of the famous houses, or temporary leaders. That meant this Mischer was one of the latter. In other words, that he was a resourceful, talented man who had to be watched at all times.

But he couldn't sit here pondering Mischer forever.

ADMINISTRATOR

"What is the purpose of your visit?" Sei asked in an over-friendly voice
as he accepted a thick sheaf of documents from the representatives. "I
imagine if you've all come together like this, it must be pretty important,
right?"

"..."

No one replied.

Sei softened his voice another notch, and said, almost laughing, "Has
your Administrator done something wrong? Or is there some totally in-
soluble problem?"

The representatives exchanged glances, and at last the eldest, the representative from the Central Islands, urged him on.

"For the time being, won't you please read the documents?"

"Oh, I see..."

Sei turned the page with his finger, and scanned it. As he read it, he recognized it. He had already read one just like it.

Right.

It was identical to the "demand" presented to the Administrator who had
been here before Sei came. The previous Administrator had flatly refused
it, and stored the documents themselves in the archives. Sei had read them
there.

It was a list of demands that an Administrator had, of course, refused,
but also that the Federation itself could not possibly accept. First of all,
the nine independent governments would combine to form a single en-
tity, to be called the United States of Gun'gazen. That nation would have
total sovereignty over the Rhamphorynchus Archipelago, and would be
governed by a ruling committee... And even the Administrator would
not interfere with the decisions of the Committee. The Committee
would be headed by a single person who would create the necessary political institutions, headed by selected ministers, and the directives of the
government would take precedence over those of the robots. Not only
that. It also removed the limits on the colonists' land, giving them full
rights to the Fishing Islands, and even, depending on their needs, rights
to colonize Babel. The Administrator would give full support, including

use of the robots, for the development of the colonial world... It continued in a like vein for some time.

When the previous Administrator received this demand for the first
time, he didn't change his expression, of course, but he was struck
speechless. When he handed over the reins to Sei, he had said, with a wry
smile, "You give a little to human beings, and they keep taking more and
more and more...".

Sei understood his feelings now. Of course neither the previous Administrator, nor Sei – nor, for that matter, any Administrator – could swallow
such an audacious set of demands... And even if they did, the Central
Body of the Federation certainly wouldn't remain silent. If they were to
allow the Administration to be ignored like this, the Federation would lose
its authority in equal measure. True, the political level of this planet was at
Class v – an exceedingly free level – but, even for Class v, no self-government was permitted for a population of over two million. According to
caste sociology, levels of power elites and societal dropouts developed and
became too fixed, too prevalent. After all, famous families and academies
had already developed among the local governments here on Gun'gazen,
with urban populations of only seventy to one hundred twenty or one
hundred thirty thousand. It was just out of the question to consider a government for ten million that was not even under the control of the Administrator.

And there was more.

Among their demands, there was one that the Fishing Islands should
be opened up little by little to settlements as the population increased.
The same couldn't apply to Babel, though. Babel had been given to the
Gun'gazea from the start. Leaving aside the matter of Gun'gazea mental
development, and only considering the level of their civilization, it was
easy to see what would happen if humans were allowed unrestricted
entry into Babel. There were countless examples in human history...
Probably there would be a repetition of what had happened in America
and Asia and Africa. Plus which, hadn't the colonists themselves said,
just twenty years ago, that Babel was not fit for colonization? They had

become greedy with their industrial development, feeling a sense of confinement in the Archipelago, and lusting for the Fishing Islands, and the metal resources of the Babel continent.

However you looked at it, you could only see these demands as the result of total ignorance on the part of the colonists towards the immense power of the Federation and the Administrator System. Living for so long on this peaceful, lazy planet, they had come to think this was the standard for Administrators. Hadn't they forgotten that there had been a time when the Forces crushed rebels mercilessly? And even now, those same Forces were still waiting for the opportunity to sharpen their claws and take power again, even though they were controlled by the Central Body.

Exactly because they knew that fact so well, the previous Administrators had kicked the demand out, and Sei felt exactly the same way.

The fact was that there were worlds with governments similar to what they were demanding – with no Administrator or robots, with self-government – currently in the Federation, although they were rare. They were exceptions to the rule, and they had been made to meet a tremendous number of special conditions to achieve their special status. To imagine meeting those conditions here on Gun'gazea was...

Downright ridiculous.

For the colonists of Gun'gazen, such a time was still in the far-distant future. There was no doubt they had to consider a little more deeply about those worlds that had achieved independent status already.

How could he possibly explain all that to these representatives seated here in front of him?

Sei placed the sheaf on a side-table and faced them.

"Well? What do you say?" asked the representative from the Central Islands.

"This is the same as was submitted before," said Sei, tapping the papers lightly. "I'm sure you still recall what the previous answer was? My answer is the same."

"Why?" asked another representative.

"Why?" nodded Sei, a half-smile on his face. "The previous Administrator should have made it clear before. Must I repeat it?"

"The times have changed!" shouted yet a third representative, desperately. "Maybe it was true in the past, but this is now! Things are different!"

"Would it be possible to at least ask you to investigate it?" asked the man from the Central Islands.

"In that case, may I keep these documents?" asked Sei as he gathered them up and stood. "Still, I feel the answer will remain the same. No objections, I trust?"

The representatives began to get agitated. They finally noticed that Sei was going to end the meeting.

"One moment, please."

The man who had spoken was Mischer.

"We hate to bother you, but I wonder if we couldn't have just a little more of your time?"

"If you wish," said Sei, sitting down again. "My opinion, though, probably won't change."

"I know that," bowed Mischer. "I merely want to explain our thinking to the Administrator of this world… To you."

"Please," responded Sei, thinking that the other was going to make his opinions heard no matter what.

"We know our demands are absolutely ridiculous to you," said Mischer. "Our demands, in basic terms, are to grant Gun'gazen the rights of self-government as an independent colony world. And, for this world just granted Class V, Type A status, that right is only a dream, of the distant future."

"…"

Sei was astounded – he didn't show it, of course, but he looked at the other again. This was the first time he had even met a colonist who understood the approach of the Administrator to government so well.

"The Federation has made it a necessity for certain strict conditions to be fulfilled before granting complete independence to a colony world…

But is there really any particular need for them to treat this right as a special dispensation?"

Mischer continued to speak softly.

"There is no need for it. The Federation's Central Body, now more than ever, has become a bureaucracy, and looks upon the granting of independence as a special blessing. At the start of the Administration System, though, the final goal was to have all colony worlds controlled under a flexible system, and for each to be independent as fit its needs and possibilities. The Administrator System liberated colony worlds that had been under the military governors of the Forces, allowed them their own say in things, and worked towards making them pillars of the Federation – that was why the Administrator System was formed – it's only natural."

Sei didn't try to say anything. There was no need. Everything Mischer was saying was true. Mischer was talking exactly like an Administrator.

This man was... Sei's memory suddenly came back to him.

Mischer... Gainue.

Mischer PPKD Gainue.

Damn.

He was an Administrator. Or, rather, had been an Administrator. To finally become an Administrator, you had to pass countless tests and training without failing, as so many did. Even if you passed all the tests, and finally gained the PPKE status of an unassigned Administrator, you could still fail during field training, under the eye of an older Administrator. After all that, you were finally assigned as Administrator on a relatively easy-to-govern world somewhere. When you reached that point, you were pretty stable as an Administrator, but... There were still occasional individuals who intentionally threw away their painfully acquired status. There had been no cases during the beginning of the Administrator System, but there had been one or two a year lately. No doubt there were various reasons for them to throw their posts away, and they must have had many various thoughts, but none of it was explained to the current Administrators. Their names were simply stricken from the list.

Mischer was one of those.

The reason Sei had felt he had heard that name somewhere before was that he had seen it on the Administrator's name list many times. He could verify it later by comparing the ID number, but he could sense directly that anyone who talked like this either was an Administrator, or was someone who had close ties to an Administrator.

"We would like to see this concept realized here on our world, on Gun'gazea, at least; even though what was once the target has now become a mere reward... That is why we brought this appeal."

Mischer continued.

"We intend to continue submitting this appeal until we finally reach our goal. This is what I wished to explain to you as Administrator."

"I understand," nodded Sei. He opened his mouth to lightly counter what the other had said, then stopped. If this Mischer was an Administrator older than Sei, then he already knew exactly what Sei was thinking. It wouldn't accomplish anything to put it into words.

After the representatives had left, Sei ordered SQI to bring the records on Mischer. On colony worlds, all colonists had ID numbers as a rule, and as that number was on the visitor's list, it was easy to find the data. Over the last ten years, the colonists had come to refuse the robot censuses, and only half of them, at the most, were now recorded. The Administrator before last had tried to limit this to some extent at least by making it mandatory for anyone meeting with or having any connection with the Administrator to have a number. Both the previous Administrator and Sei had continued the policy, but Sei had lately come to wonder if it hadn't produced a kind of status distinction among the colonists. The fact was that the representatives today, and the important business leaders in all fields, had numbers, but their nameless underlings involved in smuggling were all unregistered.

Sei glanced over Mischer's personal file.

There was no mistake.

Mischer had quit as Administrator at twenty-six, and had come to Gun'gazen as an ordinary colonist. There was no data concerning why he had quit.

What was going on here?

Sei continued to look over Mischer's record with surprise... It was impressive. Sei picked up only the major items. Settled on Ear Island in the Archipelago at twenty-six. Became a leader of the Unification movement at twenty-nine, at thirty-two was elected as sector representative as well as head of Ear Island.

Became a member of the Kata Island Industrial Promotion Council at thirty-five, and made the Kata Island inter-island trade figures immensely profitable over the next few years. At forty he became commander of the Kata Island Defense Corps. At forty-five he was the member of the Back Island representatives responsible for communication with other governments. In order to solve the problem of inter-island fishing rights, he convened the first nine-government meeting, and then proceeded to create a super-council that could even be called the Rhamphorynchus Federation. This functioned under the Administrator for a while, during which time he was appointed as a member of the United States of Gun'gazen Preparatory Council. Now, at forty-nine, he was the First Representative of Kata Island.

Before he slept that day, Sei thought about Mischer quite a lot.

Why had he quit as Administrator? Why had he become a mere colonist? Sei, of course, couldn't imagine.

The only thing that was clear was that Mischer YF Gainue – and Mischer PPKD Gainue – were the same, and that since he had become a colonist, he had risen to a become major leader in a mere twenty years. In Terran time, of course: the colonists generally solved the time problem by counting one Terran year for each half-year on Gun'gazen. Considering that the various families were all jockeying for power, you could only call it incredible. Maybe he had revealed his past to the colonists and had used it to gain his position, but even so, to have come so far was a bit unusual.

Now that he had come out on top of the colonists, what did Mischer plan to do?

And furthermore... Sei was in the position of having to oppose him.

That had been their first meeting, thought Sei as he felt the craft begin to wing over the straits. Only a little more than a month later, they had met again. Hadn't that conversation fostered a strange, inexplicable weariness in Sei?

It had been – but Sei couldn't continue thinking.

SQ2A began speaking in its own voice.

"SQ1 wishes to communicate."

"OK."

The robot began speaking in a slightly changed voice.

"I will now report on the current status of the colonial fleet," SQ1 said. "The fleet has begun to move towards Babel continent as predicted. However, ten of the fifty ships have not moved, and are still in the South Bay of Hawke Island. It is unclear what their goal is. The defense line held by the LQS-class robots is along the course of those forty ships, which should be rendered powerless approximately ten kilometers out to sea from the Babel coastline."

"Satisfactory. If you receive any further information about those remaining ten ships, contact me at once."

"Understood."

After a fractional pause, SQ1's voice continued.

"One more point. There is a highly unusual incident to report."

"What happened?"

"A passenger vessel with almost two thousand colonists on board is approaching Unity Island. According to the report of LQQ8 on patrol, they are all armed, so I dispatched SQ2D and his group to question them on their purpose. They replied that they are a volunteer army."

"Volunteer army?"

"Yes. They explained that they respect the Administrator and have sworn loyalty to him. They want to build a fort on Unity Island to defend you from the rebel army."

"Rebel army!?"

"According to their statements, the rebel army disguised as a smuggling fleet should rendezvous at Hawke Island, set forth for Babel, then turn and land on Unity Island to attack the Administration Complex."

" . . . "

Sei had absolutely no idea how to interpret this, either.

"Their statements and the actions of the fleet have points in common, and must be considered possible," continued SQ1. "For this reason, I have intensified observation of the fleet while at the same time permitting the so-called volunteer army to continue and land on Unity Island. Naturally, the defenses of the Administration Complex are of sufficient strength even if the fleet should prove to be a rebel army, and therefore the volunteer army is unneeded. However, if I ordered this self-proclaimed volunteer army to return home as unneeded, it might well cause them to waver, and possibly even enter the rebel camp. For this reason, while I am taking precautions against the potential rebels, I have decided to allow this volunteer army to do what they wish... If you have any directives to alter this policy, I will effect them immediately."

"No. It's fine as is."

There didn't seem to be much else to do at the moment. Sei started to add "for the moment" to SQ1, then stopped.

"In that case, I will make contact again if there is any change in status, " added SQ1, and cut the communication.

Sei leaned against the seat and watched the sea beneath the window. There seemed to be a wind, and there were many whitecaps. His thoughts were shaking, too, much as the unstable waves. These strange events... Something was happening, but he didn't know what, yet. He'd have to analyze things as soon as he got back. He didn't know if it would tell him anything or not, but he had to try.

Sei pushed the window-shutter button, and closed his eyes.

Just before he fell asleep, he felt his thoughts drifting freely here and there, finally becoming enwrapped in a thick green-brown darkness. When that happened, he dimly perceived that he was about to fall asleep.

When his nerves were overtense, the image in his mind returned to reality once or twice, resolving into a clear, precise feeling of dread. He would lie in bed with his eyes open, realizing he had woken up again.

Like now.

The blankness Sei was staring into now was lit by perfect indirect lighting, the spray of its not-quite-visible radiance making the room a light darkness. SQ2B, who managed the visitors' rooms and his, had dimmed the lights for Sei. As long as the Administrator didn't touch a certain switch near his pillow, they would remain that way. Even if SQ1 communicated an urgent message, that darkness would persist until the Administrator himself requested a change.

Habit was a strange thing, thought Sei.

As Administrator, Sei had of course studied the history of the robots that supported the Administrator System. Over the seventy years of the System, SQ1, as the epitome of all the robots, had changed from being a mobile unit into the giant monster that was now buried deep below the Administration Complex... But SQ1 had never lost its unique character. As a result, SQ1's sub-robots had been developing along an irreversible course. SQ2 and SQ3, which had originally been designed to assist SQ1 in command, gradually came to be directly responsible for the Administrator's safety as SQ1 lost its mobility. For example, defense of the Administrator outside the Complex and translation functions were the duties of SQ2A, while SQ2B watched over him when he was inside. Now both were designed to receive orders from SQ1, but they were assigned robots under their own direct control and could move by themselves. In other words, by parceling out its jobs among the SQ2-class robots, SQ1 had freed itself to handle more complex work than in the past. At the same time, the LQ-class robots that used to work near the Administrator had been banished to the far perimeter, where they were allowed major duties. It was much the same as in the ancient Imperial courts, where kinship ties between the nobles and the Imperial bloodline grew thinner and thinner, and nobles became more powerful on the frontiers. At the same time, the nobility at court came to the forefront of power. It was the same phenomenon.

Naturally, there had been good reasons for it. It could be said that the positions of the highly capable LQ-class robots had been usurped by the SQ2-class, which held the wishes of the Administrator as their highest priority. In any case, it had reached this pattern now. The Administrator, who knew all of this, watched it silently, as it was not only highly useful, but good for his pride, too. Sei laughed cynically at himself for that sense of usefulness and for not doubting that it was for his benefit, even now.

Still... His consciousness of it was a mere wisp of fog in the back of his mind.

He was playing in his memories now. He was recalling his meeting with Mischer YF Gainue... With Mischer PPKD Gainue.

He wondered if you could really call it a meeting...

It was the second time they had met, half a year ago (or a year, by Terran reckoning), a non-official meeting in the largest city of this world, in the Rhamphorynchus Archipelago.

The music had grown quiet. It was tired, but it still continued. The brilliant chandelier that had been attracting stares up to an hour ago had dimmed, and was coalescing into dully shining shadows at the edges of his vision.

The only person sitting in front of Sei was Mischer. Sei didn't know if it had happened that way by accident, or if the colonists arranged it on purpose. In any case, the party was still not over yet, people were clustered off in the distance, laughing and whispering together. Among those men and women of the upper crust, in their elegant attire, a slow, languid feeling drifted. The colonists gathered here were all of the top class – they all had wealth or power or rank or were merely famous – and maybe it was reasonable they should all be so languid. Mischer, of course, was no exception.

They were both silent. Maybe it would be better to say that both were aware that the others had left, and each was waiting for the other's opening gambit.

Sei had tried explaining his opinions to many of the colonists, and had been rebuffed with painfully hard counters.

Sei wasn't the host here. He hadn't even been invited. He had simply showed up at one of the regular social parties of the ruling class. Sei knew he wasn't likely to be greeted warmly. He knew it, but as Administrator he had to find out if they really knew exactly what they were doing, if they knew how close they were to a violent reaction: with all their intensified smuggling, their anti-robot sentiments, their growing independence and unification movements – the "United States of Gun'gazen"... It was difficult to do officially, and all the harder for the colonists' stubbornness. At an official meeting, their actions were all recorded, and he was forced to go by the book. He might even have to use force to make them recognize his position. If he had to drop the hammer on them, then he would first have to inform the Federation, and issue an Emergency Condition order to SQI. If he did those things, then he wouldn't be able to stop in midstream. Before he went that far, Sei wanted to try correcting their views unofficially.

First of all, wasn't it his right and obligation to monitor the colonists and their world? To some extent, Sei was berating himself for his own indecisiveness. He had avoided this type of contact because he wanted to avoid exciting them needlessly. Things had developed to the point where he had no choice, now. In general, colonists welcomed a visit by their Administrator, certainly without any hatred. That was simply the way relations were between colonists and Administrators. In principle... And, in truth, the robots reported that there were a few friendly colonists, awaiting stronger contacts with the Administrator. Insofar as that attitude didn't prevail here, it demonstrated the complexity of this colony world's problems... No, of the Administrator System itself.

As he had expected, he was received respectfully, and coldly. Sei en-

tered the salon with only sq2a — which was itself more than enough to
anger them — and had started various conversations to blend in, conversations that would not offend anyone. Finally, he began on the real subject… That he wanted them to stay as colonists under the rule of the
Federation, under its regulations. If they didn't, forcible means would
become necessary. He asked them to please reconsider their actions.

There was no response.

Or rather, their answer was a deliberate lack of response. Sei's words
had been completely expected, and while they wouldn't counter him to
his face, they certainly had no intention to follow his requests.

And was Mischer the same?

The music was still continuing. Not a tape, but a live band. Sei honestly
couldn't deny that this salon and these people were elegant and fascinat-
ing. To Sei, their parties were highly reminiscent of what he knew of
nineteenth century Europe.

But what… What, asked his heart, what was this beauty? This beauty
was merely honoring the accumulation of wealth. It was a splendor that
would produce nothing more. Wasn't it merely the glitter of apparent
authority, actually nothing but using people, squeezing the land, controlling the channels of distribution, carefully built organizations? Sei knew
that this splendor held a hard-to-resist fascination, a resplendence. This
beauty was never found outside these surroundings, for example, in a
public building, or a huge computer center built for the people. There
everything was highly functional, too empty, too sharp. Sei looked on
that emptiness and sharpness as a sign that new life was buried inside,
and that there was still hope left in some form. To Sei, whether or not
that hope existed was a major problem, and regardless of how gorgeous
everything looked to him now, he could not permit himself to sink into it.

"I wonder if it's all right to speak?" asked Mischer, looking at Sei.

"Please forgive me that my manner of speaking is not that of the
colonists," said Mischer, speaking softly. "Still, talking this way allows me
to express myself freely, and you needn't fear baring your teeth, either."

He suddenly laughed.

"Actually, I'm hoping we might talk as two Administrators together. You're a rank C, while I ended at rank D, and now I'm nothing at all... Do I offend you?"

"Not particularly."

Under normal circumstances, this was an unimaginable event... But now, it might be the easiest way, thought Sei as he answered. Maybe the reason he felt so little resistance to Mischer was that he hadn't talked freely with another human being for such a long time.

"That's good," said Mischer, switching his gaze directly to Sei. "Well? I don't think you're still looking at Gun'gazen as the same collective colony it was in the past."

"Keep talking," pressed Sei, deliberately being a little rude.

"We're not, you know. Government has become absolutely necessary here; we've reached that point."

"Government? There's government in a society of two people."

"I'm not talking about that sort of concept."

"Well, what are you talking about?"

"You think you know government inside out. You're an Administrator. With power behind you, it's easy to rule by issuing orders, using coercion, and that works in simply constructed groups. When the group exceeds a certain size, a certain level of complexity in inter-relations – in other words, a high-level society – that type of rule becomes impossible. You agree?"

"You're right, but what of it?"

"To give an example, think of an army. Even in such a perfectly strict organization, the army stops functioning as the commander wishes when the functions of its separate elements become too diverse."

"Probably," nodded Sei. "But it's the Federation that decides whether or not a colony world has reached that stage. Until it reaches that stage, it is under Administration... You should understand that much, at least."

"In a healthy system, yes," replied Mischer, smiling with the special smile of a middle-aged man full of self-confidence. That Mischer should wear such a cheerful expression at such a time!

"However, as I pointed out before when we met with all of the representatives, that mechanism is not functioning normally any longer. No, it would be better to say that it is not being carried out, as it includes a certain degree of human intention. At the moment, hasn't it become a special gift for a colony world to be separated from the rule of the Administrator? As an Administrator, of course you can't state your agreement, but a fact is a fact. For that reason, a number of colony worlds are in trouble. To be blunt, a number of the worlds being ruled by the glorious Administrators under the protection of the Federation have become, for exactly that reason, ungovernable by the Administrator System. That is what I think. And this world is one of them."

"Mischer, are you trying to make me believe that it can't be helped, even when I fail? That it's unavoidable?"

"No, why should I try such a thing? You will keep trying to the very end, I'm sure. You will because you're an Administrator."

Mischer slumped his shoulders. His face was turned away from the light, into a silhouette.

"At any rate, this colony world of ours, Gun'gazen, has become ungovernable by your methods. Needs outside your system have developed."

"Like what?"

"Status."

"Status?"

"Yes. A clear, unmistakable statement of social status, and recognition."

" . . . "

"I don't plan to argue about the techniques of government," added Mischer, turning his face back to the light. "You Administrators are the cream of the crop, superior. But isn't that superiority supported by your techniques and your knowledge? You have no knowledge of the conditions of the ruled, the experience of living tens of years on this colony world and rubbing shoulders every day with the colonists, living their everyday lives. Correct?"

"It's not important, because Administrators are as they are, and the system has come to be supported in that way."

"Wait a minute. What I want to say is exactly what that accumulation of small, apparently trivial experiences gives birth to. This foolish everyday living is the life of the colonists... It gives them a clear, solid position within their world, and a silent mutual recognition of each other. Have you ever thought about how that operates?"

"That is a point that only applies to a particular colony world."

"Exactly, exactly," nodded Mischer to himself. "As any Administrator knows, the principles of Administration are for the colonists and the native inhabitants, for both, not for either. The Administrator must never align himself with one or the other, always maintaining his logical viewpoint. For exactly that reason, the Administrator is excluded from the local society as soon as the colonists develop to a certain point and feel a sense of unity as a single world. The delicate and skillfully camouflaged thread of humanity binding Administrator and colonist breaks. After that point, what moves the colonists must be, not a mere figurehead, but a force from within their group."

"Haven't you oversimplified a bit?"

"I agree. But your mode of government has its limits, and I want you to understand that this is what I firmly believe. In a short time, Gun'gazen will no longer be amenable to rule by outsiders' theories, and outsiders' techniques. A system of rule that can function in more complex, more difficult, more indirect ways is needed."

"I see."

Sei was a little disgusted. This was merely a question of how you viewed the problem, and of course he had no choice but to defend the course he had to take as Administrator. He tried to change topics.

"And you are that true leader, I gather, with the weapons of your techniques learned as Administrator and your status as one of the colonists," said Sei, looking at the other. "So that's why you quit and came here to Gun'gazen, to test your theories?"

Mischer laughed, a little loudly.

"You try to place me so quickly. Human beings aren't like that."

"So that was why you revealed yourself so surprisingly," continued Sei relentlessly. "And somehow your ideas have become the basic ideals of the independence movement. But how long will it continue?"

"It doesn't matter."

"What?"

"Just wait a bit," said Mischer, quietly sipping the drink he had put down before. "At any rate, what I'm saying is just my – and the colonists' – thinking. But you're an Administrator, and as such you'll try to destroy what we're trying to do. Maybe you will in the end. However... Even if you do, you must know how difficult your position will become. The contradictions inherent in your function will cause it. The Administrator must work for the colony world, for the world. That is the most basic order. Even if the initial stages have the colonists weak and the natives of low civilization, you must realize that the future will bring a confrontation when both have become powerful. The Administrator himself forces it. What becomes of the Administrator in that situation? The Administrator is facing both sides; both the colonists and the natives... Like Janus, the two-faced god. But can he continue that double-faced existence? It's probably occurred to you, but as Administrator, you must hold both positions to fulfill both goals... So what to do? That's what's happening on Gun'gazen. You're bound... You're on the boundary itself... And isn't it merely a matter of time to see which way you jump?"

Mischer shrugged his shoulders, and leaned back into the seat.

"That got pretty long, sorry – I just said what I've heard... Forgive me."

Mischer suddenly changed his tone as he noticed two or three party-goers approaching.

"Are you still in conference?" asked a young girl lightly, sitting down next to Mischer.

"The Administrator speaks bluntly, and Mischer has been a man who hates to lose for a long time."

The man who spoke, and stressed the words "long time" was an elder statesman of the family that had controlled politics on the Central Islands for many generations. "Well, I believe the Administrator will come to understand our actions... Isn't it better not to get too serious, Mischer?"

"Exactly," bowed Mischer. "And the people here have all come to feel this way."

Have come to...?

Sei glanced at Mischer again. He was smiling.

In that instant, Sei understood.

The strange feeling Sei had felt when he had asked how long Mischer could continue, and Mischer had replied that it didn't matter... Suddenly, it all fell into place.

Wasn't Mischer gambling? The fact that Mischer was continuing as a leader of the independence movement, knowing exactly how the colonists would appear to the Administrator and the Federation... He was gambling on that slim chance. He was striving to build up his own independent self-governed nation here on Gun'gazen, leading the blind colonists, who could only see their own interests, not telling them of the danger.

Maybe he was wrong in his analysis of Mischer.

Maybe he was just thinking too much.

But it certainly seemed possible. At any rate, it was something that Administrator Sei could well understand. It was certainly possible for Mischer, if he decided to become a real leader among the colonists. Mischer was trying to prove the validity of his thinking.

That was an extremely "anti-Administrator" position, but wasn't it – at the same time – precisely the same feeling as that held by the Administrator himself?

He felt a weird, formless sympathy with Mischer... But maybe it was all Sei's misreading.

Hmm...

Hadn't he fashioned his own illusions and then been waiting for them to appear?

What had the colonists done after that unofficial meeting? If, as he had thought before, it could be called a meeting.

After that event, the very substance of the smuggling changed, resistance to the arresting robots increased, and human casualties began appearing. And hadn't those strange handbills begun appearing after that, and the illegal broadcasts slipped into the colonists' radio programs? Even though the robots had tried, they had never been able to locate or arrest more than the drones, just the low-level operators. Strange broadcasts – saying things like *The robots are not working for the benefit of the colonists. As proof*, it went on, *hadn't they killed, and wouldn't they continue to kill?* Ridiculous broadcasts, saying that the robots eliminated humans as mere objects, not treating them as humans, in the pursuit of their duties... It had all started after that meeting.

However he looked at it, it seemed that the instigators of the movement were among the colonists themselves, the upper levels of leaders among the colonists. The robots' analysis bore him out. In addition, there was the problem that Mischer was among them... Or rather, that Mischer was pulling the strings. He strongly suspected that Mischer was behind the destruction of the robots, and the smuggling, and also those ridiculous broadcasts.

As for himself... Was he, perhaps, assigning too much weight to Mischer's past as an Administrator? Was it a mistake – not to think that, as an ex-Administrator, Mischer would choose a more intelligent, more productive course? Now, the colonists... The Mischer-controlled colonists, that is... They were probably trying out the old time-tested methods, or if not, then a low-effect approach.

Has Mischer, then, really abandoned his memories as an Administrator? Has he become a mere colonist? Sei wondered. Was it really reasonable to expect Mischer to give him so much trouble, even occasionally?

No.

Sei suddenly sat up in bed. He had noticed something.

The relationship between Mischer and... SQI.

Wasn't the vague unease felt by Sei towards SQI actually being driven, deliberately, by Mischer?

SQI was, naturally, fulfilling all of its functions.

Today, SQ1 had reported the situation to him, and had taken care of it. After Sei had returned to the Complex, he had questioned SQ1 about the movement of the fleet.

Forty ships of the original fifty were still continuing towards the defensive line held by the robots off the east coast of Babel. The remaining ten ships were still at anchor in the south bay of Hawke Island. The self-proclaimed volunteer army had landed on Unity Island, and set up defenses in the middle of a fairly small desert. Nothing else had changed. The entire situation itself was extremely strange, but it was still progressing as SQ1 had predicted.

SQ1 also had another bit of information.

The Inspector's starship was approaching the system, and would probably land in a day or two. Sei had no idea what kind of person the Inspector was, or what his schedule was, but there was no mistake that he represented the Central Body of the Federation, and that he wanted to uncover his, the Administrator's, errors. That's what most of the Inspectors were now. That was probably because the Federation had recognized the huge authority that accompanied the position, and the various attractions of the subject worlds, and had therefore evaluated the Inspectors closely and trained them thoroughly. As a result, a special type of person had emerged as Inspector, and no other type was ever seen.

At any rate, Sei had good reason to be apprehensive about the Inspector's visit. It was a fact that the situation here on Gun'gazen was not just bad, but had become downright terrible. Even if he should try to pull the wool over the Inspector's eyes, it was unlikely to work. Quite the opposite: by explaining the situation fully, he might be able to make the other recognize the difficulty faced by the Administrator. And if he were censured for that, well, it was just unavoidable. He was thinking about it rationally, but the reason he could was that on countless other colony worlds there were similar problems, and government was becoming more and more difficult and unsteady everywhere, not just here on Gun'gazen. You could go so far as to say that Gun'gazen was slightly, just slightly worse than the average. If Sei was censured for it, then the same punishment would have to be meted out to a great many other Administrators as well, and he doubted the Administrator System could survive it.

Probably this kind of thinking would have been impossible for an Administrator of twenty or thirty years ago. Twenty years before, the situation of an Administrator being driven into a corner itself would have been remarkably rare. Of course, Sei didn't know from personal experience, but the records showed that if any world in the past had approached a critical level, as it had on Gun'gazen, then an ace Administrator had been dispatched to deal with it. Now, though, he was being forced to function at a level above his capacity. After all, he was assigned to this world as PPKC, not PPKA. Maybe it had become that much harder to turn out high-quality Administrators. The age when talented individuals who could have succeeded in any field yearned to become Administrators had ended, the position of the Administrator had become a mere concept, and the levels of society that should have been supplying new cadets was fast solidifying. No... Even if they repaid nothing to the Administrators, it was all still due to the fact that the Central Body and the Administrator System itself had begun to totter...

Sei cut off that line of thought. Where in the world had he picked up this habit of jumping from sidetrack to sidetrack?

Hadn't he been thinking about SQI?

Right.

If Mischer was still using his faculties developed as an Administrator... And if he was the actual power behind the colonists... Then wasn't it reasonable to assume that there was a different motive behind that ridiculous "independence" movement of the colonists?

He began to mull that over.

For example, the hysteric shooting of the robots... That appeared to be an appeal to the colonists, but couldn't it also be interpreted as a demand to SQI?

Sei had to consider what effect that would have on SQI – knowing the colonists believed that, rather than assisting them, the robots were actually murdering the colonists. Anyone who had been an Administrator for any length of time soon learned the significance of SQI. Assuming that Mischer knew it too, then it was only natural he should attempt to weaken the Administrator by striking an invisible blow at SQI's stability. Was there any way to affect an SQI as good as this one? Wouldn't SQI, trapped between its duty and the responses of the colonists, become aware of this total lack of correspondence between its judgments and the results of its actions? And the only outlet for all of SQI's perplexity — if you could think of a robot's problems that way — was the Administrator. The gap between the data banks and the actual colonists, even being called a murderer for fulfilling its duty... Wouldn't SQI begin to ask the Administrator to approve its judgments and counter-actions?

Sei was covered with cold sweat, sitting up in bed.

Wasn't that exactly what SQI was doing now?

No.

Not only that.

The rendezvous of the colonial fleet... True, it was an unusual case, but there wasn't going to be any immediate combat... Wasn't the fact that SQI had used the emergency signal a sign of just how far its distortion had gone?

And, to an SQI in that condition, Sei had asked constantly, as if not trusting the strength of the data, whether SQI had taken Mischer's presence in the Independence movement into account.

That in itself must have had an effect on SQI.

In other words, Sei had been following Mischer's strategy all along, unknowingly. Or, if you preferred, SQI was beginning to alter under the pressures of the battle between the current Administrator and the ex-Administrator.

Sei still didn't know what would happen. Still, unknowing, but possessed of a little more insight into the problem, Sei lay back on the bed... His eyes still wide open.

He slept, eventually.

− 4 −

When he woke up, it was dawn. Sei ordered SQ2B to open up the windows, changed into his uniform, and listened to SQ1's report.

"The fleet of forty colonial ships has reached the sea near the coast of Babel, and made contact with the LQS-class robots."

"And?"

"As the colonists continued to attempt to forcibly penetrate the defense line, the LQS robots are carrying out the destruction of the vessels' propulsion systems as planned. Shall I display a live broadcast on your private screen?"

"No. Send it to the screen in the office. I'll take it there."

"Understood."

SQ1 fell silent, and Sei got into the elevator.

When he entered his bright, sunlit office, the dark thoughts that had tormented him during the night seemed like a dream. Weren't they, after all, just worrying too much? Wasn't this instant, what he was doing, the Complex, wasn't everything exactly as usual? Everything was operating normally, under the appropriate policies. The work of the Administrator was being carried out efficiently. So what was bothering him?

When Sei sat down in his chair and looked at the screen, the situation began to look a little less pleasant.

The colonial ships were scattered across the screen, including some that were quite large. At a glance, over half of them had already had their engines smashed, and were drifting. Above the ships still under power, the LQS robots, with their blue-black wide-spread wings, were diving down to attack, then folding their wings and climbing on gravity propulsion, then falling to another target. It was a spectacle that must have made the colonists feel they were under attack by a host of demons.

Seen on the screen, it somehow failed to appear real.

Still, it does impart the advantage of being able to view the situation objectively, thought Sei, as he squinted his eyes. Just as he thought that, one of the LQS robots lost control, and plummeted towards the sea.

Magnetic resonators.

The colonists has begun to use the magnetic resonators!

"Idiots! What are you doing!?" shouted Sei. As he shouted, what he had feared came to pass. The robot smashed into the sea with a huge water-spout, and then its gravity propulsion system exploded with a flare of light. A number of nearby ships twisted as if hit, and began to sink. "It's... It's suicidal!" Sei bellowed.

The colonists, though, made no effort to stop. The drifting ships began to fire their deck-mounted magnetic resonators at the LQS robots, and the smaller ships continued to fire their lasers – even though the robots they picked off then plunged into the sea and exploded, sinking ships each time. The colonists continued to fire. They were resisting as if possessed, even though they knew further resistance might cost their lives.

It was a blind resistance born of terror. It was a scream to drive away those monsters in the sky – if needed, to be blasted by their explosions in the sea – anything was better than to be continuously attacked from above. If the planners of this attack – those who had deployed the fleet – had actually planned that far... It was a plan of unholy skill. As he stared, yet another LQS robot fell and sank, together with a colonial vessel, after exploding.

Already, how many colonists had died, wondered Sei, and shivered. The colonists would say they had all been murdered.

"Tell the LQS robots to..."

Even as he began to order them pulled back, SQ1 had already issued the order. The robots floating in the sky drifted away from the reach of the colonial disruptors, and began to regroup.

And...

Sei doubted what he was seeing.

The ships that still had engines chased after the robots ferociously. When the robots pulled still further back, the ships pursued again, firing every weapon they possessed. Naturally, the ships could not hope to catch the flying robots, but they seemed determined to follow them for-ever.

"They're insane," Sei said softly, unconsciously standing up.

He couldn't believe that what they were doing was a rational act. They were motivated only by their hatred of the robots, in spite of the fact that it was flatly impossible to destroy them all, no matter how hard they tried... They carried the fight to the robots, knowing they might die for it. At least, that was all that Sei could imagine.

Sei calculated at full speed exactly what the result of this would be.

In this combat, dozens, hundreds of colonists must have died. Of course, his side had lost a lot, too, but robots were only robots, not people. Among the colonists, the image of the robots as mass-murderers would settle firmly, and their hatred and fear would rise like a flood. In addition, the original plan was to tow back the disabled ships and question the crews, but now that they had displayed such hysteria, it had become flatly impossible even to approach them. If a robot tried to approach, it would be shot down by that illegal weapon, the magnetic resonator. When that happened, there would be another explosion, more deaths. And while he was doing that, the colonists floating in the ocean would be drowning one by one. It looked like there was no way for the colonists to save themselves, either.

If he let things ride, more colonists would die, causing the Archipelago to view him as an enemy, actively disobey, and rebel against him. It was clear that the leaders of the Independence movement would use that enmity to stir up a full-scale insurrection. He had to avoid that at all cost.

Sei bit his lip.

The fact that SQ1 had still not yet commented must have been because it was still weighing the pros and cons of what it could do within the range of its permissible actions.

For the moment, he had to save as many colonists as possible, decided Sei. Save as many as possible now, and figure out what to do with them later.

"Prepare life rafts," he said. "Drop them from high altitude."

"Understood," answered SQ1 at once. Sei didn't know if SQ1 was satisfied with that answer, or put at ease. At any rate, it carried out the order at once.

As soon as the group of cargo robots left the Complex, SQ1 conveyed a totally unexpected bit of news.

A number of Gun'gazea had appeared on the coastline, and were making preparations to try to rescue the colonists.

Sei was speechless for a moment.

It wasn't, strictly speaking, impossible. He didn't know which group it was, but it wasn't unlikely that they had been given radios. It was hardly strange they should set out in rescue boats in response to the colonists' communication. Still, Sei had never thought that it might happen. Even though some smugglers might have that sort of relationship with some nations, he never thought that the Gun'gazea would display so openly that they were engaged in smuggling. And that they should do it in spite of the fact that the colonists had fired on the robots, which was forbidden... Sei felt a dull, deep pain in his heart.

Was he... Was the Administrator now respected so little? Had he become that kind of figure for both the colonists and the Gun'gazea? Had the Gun'gazea, too, gone that far?

Mischer's words and the words of the D'o of Kuwast come back to him, together.

When the Administrator, the two-faced god, can't satisfy both, then what happens?

You and your robots are always impartial. Leaving aside for the moment the point of whether it's actually possible or not...

They were right.

The past Administrators had given careful thought to the contact of the Gun'gazea and the colonists, and had restricted it... And had come to believe that restriction was needed... But wasn't that about to end? Weren't they at the stage where the Administrator shouldn't interfere: fighting together, communicating as they were now?

No! Sei opened his eyes.

Not yet.

Looking at it objectively, they hadn't come that far yet. He believed it. And he was the Administrator.

He could not back down, he could not allow the colonists and the Gun'gazea to mingle like this.

Before it was too late…

Before it was too late, yes, he had to stop those Gun'gazea. He had to convince them, or stop them by force if needed… he had to make them withdraw. Even if he became isolated from both the colonists and the Gun'gazea, he still had to make a start somewhere.

For now, there was no choice but to order the robots on the scene to stop the Gun'gazea boats, and in the time so gained, he would have to fly to meet them, and personally convince them.

Having decided, he immediately issued the orders and went into action.

The dunes of the scorching desert streamed by beneath the window of the aircraft. They caught the morning sun, glowing yellow. They were crossing the fairly small desert in the south of Unity Island. Still, exactly because it was here on the same island as the Complex, the hand of civilization had touched it, as it had not touched Babel. There were artificial oases everywhere, and roads stretching between them. The silver flashes on the roads were the robot buses connecting the various facilities on the island with the Administration Complex.

Then he could see countless people wearing multi-colored clothes, and their tents along the coast. They were armed with rough, police-level weapons, and were walking around or sitting in their camp. Even without seeing the unfamiliar vessel moored in the harbor, he knew at once this was the "volunteer army" that SQ1 had permitted to land. They firmly believed the fleet that had assembled at Hawke Island was going to attack the Administration Complex and had come to protect it. Even if it were so, it was ludicrous to think that this motley, underarmed mass could fight anything. It was impossible that the Complex would fall to that fleet, even if the volunteer army should be defeated.

The reason Sei could see them so clearly, even without using the observation screen, was that the craft dropped down, slowed, and circled several times over their heads. The men and women of the "volunteer army" cheered and waved their arms. After that, the craft rose, and took the direct course that would take him to Babel in just a little over an hour.

"Was that directed by SQ1?" asked Sei shortly.

"Yes. Is there anything...?" replied SQ2, seated at his side. "No. Nothing," countered Sei. He felt there was no need to do anything like that for this "volunteer army", but he didn't want to listen to SQ1's long explanation about it. It was already done.

He felt himself grow depressed. SQ1 had never before given that kind of directive, even when Sei had first come to Gun'gazen. To think that SQ1 was respecting the feelings of the colonists to that point... Hadn't that broadcast being circulated to the colonists entered SQ1's data banks, and affected it after all? Hadn't SQ1, in other words, significantly changed?

Leave it alone.

Sei drove away those thoughts that came bubbling up within him.

The sea unfolded beneath him.

"There is a communication from SQ1," said SQ2 suddenly.

"What?"

"Hold on please..." The voice changed into SQ1's. "LQQ5A and LQQ44A that were near the area have stopped the Gun'gazea from making preparations to rescue the colonists."

"Stopped? By persuasion or by force?"

"For the moment, by persuasion. However, both LQQ5A and LQQ44A are surveying robots, and therefore their command of spoken Gun'gazea is very limited. In addition, as I cannot take over their speakers and communicate directly, it is only a matter of time before they will be required to use force to stop them."

"I understand."

"LQQ5A has managed to determine which group it is. According to its report, they are Cotoru."

"Cotoru?"

Sei's eyes narrowed.

Cotoru was one of the nations trying to crush Kuwast, wasn't it? The

Kuwast D'o had said that the Cotoru and the Toka had received highly advanced weaponry through smuggling... Which meant they had a need to try to rescue the colonists, even though they had attacked the robots in broad daylight.

"Aren't the Cotoru based a little further south?"

"Yes, but nonetheless, they are there now," responded SQI. "It appears they came for smuggling and were waiting there."

"Hmm..."

"There is another report," continued SQI. "The ten ships moored in the south bay of Hawke Island have begun to move."

"Move? Where to?"

"It is still unclear. I will communicate as soon as I know."

"As soon as possible."

SQI cut the communication.

So the remaining ten ships had begun to move...

To where?

Were they following the other forty to Babel? Or were they withdrawing to the Archipelago? Or did they really intend to attack the Administration Complex as the "volunteer army" said?

He didn't know.

He didn't know, but... In any case, he had to let it ride for now. How, he had to make the Gun'gazea – the Cotoru – stop trying to rescue the colonists.

His craft flew over the colonists' fleet at a high altitude. In this clear weather he would certainly be seen, but there was no point in – or need to – avoid it now. As long as they couldn't reach him with their magnetic resonators, that was sufficient. He observed them carefully through the screen, and could see the countless drifting ships, and the dozens of life-rafts dropped by the cargo robots. There were colonists riding in the life-rafts. For now, that was enough.

He finally arrived on Babel. Where the jungle ended and changed to beach, the craft hovered down neatly.

Two robots flew up to meet him, and then landed flanking him. Of course, they were LQQ5A and LQQ44A.

The first to step out of the craft was SQ2A. After SQ2A had exchanged data with the other two robots, it turned to Sei.

"They are saying that they absolutely must set out to sea."

Sei got out of the aircraft.

In front of him, six or seven metal and wood constructions that could only be called boats were lined up at the water's edge, each capable of carrying maybe ten passengers. As if to protect them, twenty or thirty Gun'gazea were gathered in front, watching him. A number were carrying guns, and the rest had shining blue swords at their sides. Side-lit by the sun, they all looked incredibly fierce.

"The Administrator has come!" blasted SQ2A at full volume.

The Gun'gazea jumped, startled, and then as one of them fell to his knees the others followed suit. It showed that his title still held the same authority it had held in the past.

Then one of them rose, bowed quickly, and ran off into the forest. Immediately, a single D'o heading a number of Gun'gazea come forth. The D'o's skin was of woven gold and black.

As usual, SQ2A translated.

"This is the first time we have met... They say you are the Administrator?" asked the D'o in its unique high-pitched speech, looking at Sei as if trying to humor him.

Sei nodded.

"Yes. I am Sei PPKC Konda. I am the Administrator, as I lead the robots," he said, then paused for a moment. "Also, further proof is in the fact that they do not contradict me."

"Excuse me. Now I see," bowed the D'o. "I have only met the Administrator once, and at that time it was not you. It was your predecessor, or the one before that... I am a D'o of the Cotoru."

"My pleasure."

As he answered, Sei felt his tension rise. The fact that this D'o had only met the Administrator once showed that the nation had little connection with the Administrator or the Administration System. Even if that were merely due to chance, it still revealed that they were fairly unfriendly... In other words, it meant they were relatively independent. Which was certainly true of the Cotoru. If he wished their cooperation, he would have to exert tremendous effort. And under these strained conditions, as well.

"To get to the point, it appears you are making an attempt to set to sea." Sei felt he had to control the course of the conversation, so he began at once. "Could you please tell me why you must do so here and now?"

"To rescue humans," answered the D'o abruptly. It seemed that this D'o and his nation would be treating Sei as merely another D'o.

"People?"

"Those that live in the cold world... the colonists... seem to have had an accident. We want to rescue them."

The fact that the word "colonists" had come out was proof of this D'o's extensive contact with the people of the Archipelago through smuggling. Sei let that lie for the moment, and progressed.

"I see. But how did you discover this fact?"

"We had a communication."

"A communication? Through some machine?"

"No."

The D'o refused to say he had received a smuggled communicator.

"They were seen by some Cotoru that were afloat in the bay."

"Oh, really? In that case, those Cotoru must certainly know why the colonists are in trouble, and how they came to be there."

"I haven't any idea," said the D'o calmly. "When we saw them, it was already after whatever caused it."

It seemed he couldn't trap this one too easily. Sei changed his tactics.

"OK. Let's say it happened that way. However, you are here, away from your lands, with many Gun'gazea, many boats, and goods hidden in the trees over there. I wonder if you made all these preparations after finding out that the colonists were in difficulty."

"Am I under an obligation to respond?"

"I wonder. Didn't you assemble here for the purpose of smuggling?"

When he said that, the D'o hunched a little, and stared at Sei fixedly.

"Administrator," said the D'o, "I am talking with you as D'o to D'o. Therefore, I would like answers to my questions also."

"Do you have any questions?"

"I have. The fact that your underlings are trying to prevent our actions... Is this because of your order...?"

"Of course."

"And why are we not permitted to rescue the colonists?"

"An interesting manner of speaking. Aren't you in fact, more interested in the goods they carry than in saving their lives?"

"..."

The D'o fell silent for a moment, then spoke deliberately.

"I will permit those words because I am a magnanimous D'o. It is also a fact that the colonists may be dying even now."

"It will suffice to leave their lives to the robots. Even now, life rafts have already been dropped."

"...still..." The D'o shook his head. "We can hardly stop our attempt for that reason. We have come here as a result of a decision made by the D'o council of Cotoru... What is this?"

The D'o's shout was due to the fact that the robots following the conversation – LQQ5A and LQQ44A, and even the aircraft itself – had moved to surround the Gun'gazea, and taken positions that showed they were ready for combat.

"Oh, excuse me. I'm so sorry," said Sei quietly. "I hope I haven't offended you... At any rate, as long as I have responsibility to stop smuggling, I also have a duty to prevent you from setting out to sea. This is the duty of the Administrator... It appears that you have not considered this very deeply... But it is a fact."

"Very well. We will withdraw," said the D'o after a pause, its eyes flashing. Sei, of course, had no idea of what was bubbling up in the D'o's heart. "However," continued the D'o, "I will be unable to carry out my duty as a D'o, and will be viewed as having failed, causing this problem to be magnified many times. I request you to come to Cotoru and explain in detail to the D'o council… If you do not, we will have no choice but to fight to the death here."

"…"

Sei turned and looked at SQ2A. It appeared there was no choice but to go to Cotoru… And travel with the Cotoru was always on foot. He had to consider how long it was likely to take to get there.

SQ2A analyzed the data from LQQ5A, LQQ44A, and its own sources, and estimated the time at two hours.

Two hours.

Well, it was unavoidable.

Plus which, if he entered Cotoru, he would have a chance of finding out if the Cotoru really possessed smuggled weapons, as the Kuwast said.

He should go.

Just as he decided, SQ1 communicated. "It is now clear that the ten ships from Hawke Island are bound for Unity Island," reported SQ1. "SQ2D and its group were attacked at once when they approached to question the ships as to their destinations, so I pulled them back. Estimating that they may well land on Unity Island and attack the Administration Complex, I have taken the following actions: One, as the so-called volunteer army could well be destroyed by combat, I have made preparations to take them safely inside the Complex. Two, I have raised the emergency exterior wall around the Complex. Three, I have entered full combat status. Do you have any additions or directives?"

"That's sufficient. What about the forty ships?"

"They are still drifting. They are still prepared to resist, but there will be no further loss of life due to the life-rafts. I plan to wait another twelve hours, and them collect them as planned, when they have become tractable."

"Good. You should have received the communication from SQ2A by now, so you know I will be unable to return for two to three hours. Take full control during that time."

"Understood," answered SQ1, and then revealed its true colors. "If you will be traveling with the native inhabitants, your current protection is insufficient. For your protection, I am dispatching a platoon of fifty-one combat robots. They will take up positions above you and monitor the area."

When the communication ended, Sei faced the Gun'gazea, who were looking increasingly alarmed.

"Well, then," he pressed, "Let's be on our way to Cotoru."

It was hot.

They formed a military column.

In the front of the column were Gun'gazea carrying their trade goods, followed by the D'o and its group of bodyguard Gun'gazea. About two meters behind them came the Administrator's group, led by Sei and SQ2A. The form of the column had evolved so they could advance while watching each other. It was a design that allowed the D'o and Sei to talk to each other, while also ensuring that one could be immediately taken hostage if his side did anything wrong. The D'o had requested this arrangement. At first, the D'o had requested that Sei walk among them alone, but Sei had refused, and they had settled on this.

It was clear, though, that the Administrator had the advantage. The robots had tremendous power, not readily visible, and overhead there was the platoon of combat robots protecting him.

Whether the D'o knew all this or not, it sometimes slowed, talked to Sei, sent off runners to inform Cotoru – or so it said – and sometimes urged on the baggage carriers.

The Gun'gazea carrying the goods were chanting a monotonous melody together, repeating it. The goods were being carried in various ways; some in carts, some on the backs of the Gun'gazea, but all were covered and Sei couldn't determine the contents.

The road through the jungle was no mere path. It was a wide, hard-packed road, and it was obvious it was well-used and well-cared for. Probably it was used for smuggling... He had no complaint with the Gun'gazea building roads. The problem was that SQ2A had taken this easy-to-walk road into its calculations, which meant they still had a long way to go.

During that time, SQ1 sent another communication.

The ten ships had landed on Unity Island, and engaged in combat with the "volunteer army". The volunteers, with fewer weapons and no training, had been crushed at once, and were fleeing north. The colonists that had landed – at this point, SQ1 asked for confirmation to call them rebels – assembled some rough cars for the apparent purpose of pursuing them, so SQ1 had dispatched a dozen or so robot buses to carry the fleeing volunteers to safety inside the walls of the Administration Complex.

Sei wondered just how SQ1 planned to look after some two thousand people inside the Complex… But SQ1 must have already thought of that. Sei had no choice at the moment but to leave everything to SQ1, and dedicate his energies to the negotiations with the Cotoru. He felt a little uneasy at it, though. He was uneasy about the black-and-white contrast that SQ1 had drawn between the "rebels" and the "volunteers", but he could verify the facts himself when he returned and issue new orders if needed.

For now, it was hot. The sun piercing through the trees was hot, and the humidity was even higher than yesterday.

"Aren't you tired?" asked the D'o, slowing its pace. SQ2A translated it almost immediately.

"No. Not at all."

"Oh, I see," nodded the D'o, and continued. "I have something I would like to ask you."

"What is it?"

"Will the Administrator be on this world forever?"

"Hmm…" Sei kept his voice expressionless. "How long… Well, not forever. If the Federation so orders, I could be gone tomorrow."

The D'o looked at Sei with something like disbelief in its eyes.

"No, not that meaning. Not you personally. My question was: when will there cease to be an Administrator on this world?"

"I'm afraid I can't say."

Sei felt a bit of surprise at the other's rudeness. "And it is not a question that can be answered easily."

"At any rate, not for a long time?"

"I would expect that to be correct, yes."

"Why?"

The D'o refused to quit.

"Why must you be on this world for such a long time?"

"What do you want to say?"

"Shall I speak, then? The Administrator, from the outside, has helped Gun'gazea in many ways. New skills, new ways of thinking... We should thank you, certainly. But it is also a fact that the Administrator is helping the colonists."

"..."

Not again? thought Sei, listening.

"Thanks to the efforts of the Administrator, both the Gun'gazea and the colonists have grown greatly. At any rate, I have so heard," continued the D'o. "Isn't that enough? Hasn't this world become capable of progressing quite well without the Administrator... No, better? It is said that the Administrator himself thinks that he should yield to a successor that lives on this world, and watch and protect from his own world." He looked at Sei.

"Or maybe the Administrator doesn't have the ability to make his own decisions; I don't know. Maybe he is merely an extension of the Federation's will. A mere stand-in for distant rule."

"I have no intention to explain myself here," said Sei coldly. It seemed this D'o, or rather, that Cotoru itself had come to sympathize with the colonists, and held the same opinions. "I will speak of it in Cotoru. To all of the D'o."

"Ho-hoo..."

The D'o wanted to say something, but a runner returned just then, so it moved to the front of the column.

Sei suddenly noticed that the jungle above his head was dark and solidly overgrown. The distance between the groups had increased, too. Sei felt a sense of apprehension, especially since they had been together up until then. The road was changing to a narrower path, the growths were swelling out into the path, and Gun'gazea in front had become hidden.

"Will it still take a long time?" Sei asked SQ2A in a low voice. SQ2A replied at low volume.

"The Gun'gazea of Cotoru are leading us along a roundabout route, rather than the direct route."

"What?"

"The Cotoru may have something in mind... I cannot make a definite analysis," said SQ2A in its usual tone. "I have been trying to contact SQ1 to investigate, but SQ1's circuit has not opened for the last ten minutes, so I cannot determine SQ1's opinion."

"..."

"However, the combat robots are in position overhead, so the Administrator's safety is assured."

Sei wasn't listening, though. He was still thinking about what SQ2A had just said.

SQ1's circuits were closed?

Wasn't that impossible, especially considering SQ1's current attitude?

What was going on?

It was as if Sei's stopping was a signal. As he stopped, shouts came from the jungle on both sides. The gunshots were loud, and SQ2A issued its three kilohertz alarm signal while using its heat screen to neutralize the bullets.

Sei automatically crouched.

Again, there was the sound of bullets cutting through the air.

Screams, shouts.

"Kill him! Kill the Administrator!" translated SQ2A, and added a note of apology, "The Cotoru D'o's words..."

Simultaneously, the Gun'gazea from the front came charging back as others burst from the jungle on both sides.

Sei, still crouching, was speechless.

Was this... Was the possible?

Was it really possible that the native inhabitants could be attacking the Administrator, trying to kill him?

While Sei was frozen, though, the robots silently, quickly surrounded him and began defensive combat. A number of Gun'gazea carrying guns or flashing swords fell, torn to pieces.

Not only that.

From above, the platoon of robots came dropping down, led by their larger command robot, spitting fire left and right. One platoon of robots... Combat robots.

The combat robots had, in less than ten seconds, burned, cut, smashed, killed all the Gun'gazea in sight.

"Stop! Don't kill him! Don't kill the D'o!" shouted Sei, but he was too late. As the air cleared, all that was left was the laser-cut trees... And the mountain of corpses.

Sei stood up unsteadily.

"The command unit is apologizing for failing to fulfill your orders," reported SQ2A.

"No... No, it's all right."

He was still in shock. He still couldn't fully believe that the Gun'gazea would really try to kill him when ordered by their D'o. It had certainly been planned... That D'o had told the other Cotoru about it – the runner! – and the D'o council had decided to eliminate the problem of the Administrator, luring him to a side road and attacking him.

In other words... The Administrator meant that little to the Cotoru. The D'o council couldn't have considered whether the robots could dig out the truth of it or not... What would happen to them, finally... What the final result would be. Probably, he guessed, the colonists hadn't given that information to the Gun'gazea they had contact with.

The Cotoru had been used by the colonists! They had been used, but, as Administrator, he couldn't let it end there. He didn't want to do it, but he couldn't let groups alone that tried to harm the Administrator. He had to punish them.

Punishment.

"What about SQ1? Still no contact?" asked Sei, throwing his words like rocks.

"Not yet. Still no connection," answered SQ2A. "The circuits are still… new information… a communication has just come from SQ2D."

"From SQ2D?"

Given the way their communication system was set up, this was unheard of.

"According to SQ2D's communication, SQ1 has been destroyed," reported SQ2A in an unconcerned voice. "According to the data SQ2D has collected, it appears that the central sectors of the Administration Complex have been destroyed by explosions."

"…"

"A similar communication has just entered from SQ2E… and now from SQ2C. SQ2C reports that investigation by SQ2C3B indicates that the destruction was caused by the 'volunteer army'. Shortly before the explosions, all members of their group left, saying they intended to fight against the rebels. They forced SQ1 to lower the exterior wall and left. After the explosions, they met with and joined the rebels, and returned to the coast together. SQ2C believes this to mean that the so-called 'volunteer army' was in league with the rebels from the start."

"…"

Sei was still silent.

The shock of being attacked by the Gun'gazea had vanished. He couldn't feel its reality any more.

He wanted to say it was a lie. The robots, though, didn't lie.

He wanted to say the data was wrong. That many similar reports, though, left little chance of it.

Even so, even so…

SQ1 was… destroyed?

Wasn't that itself strictly impossible? That SQ1, the most important, most protected thing next to himself, should be destroyed?

What did it mean… Sei tried to think, confused.

If SQ1, the main support of government on this world, had been destroyed… Then, wasn't that government also destroyed? Wasn't all government now reduced to mere mechanical actions, stripped of adjustment and decision? Hadn't Gun'gazen become a world where its Administrator was totally useless? Powerless?

Yes.

Sei suddenly understood it all. He felt that all of these separate incidents welded together, revealing a single fact.

This was what the colonists had been aiming at. Mischer had manipulated the colonists, had played a strategy to reach exactly this end.

The colonists anti-robot movement... The smuggling with the Gun'gazea and their education... The strange handbills and broadcasts, all aimed at SQI... In these ways, Mischer had steered things at his own pace, slowly making SQI hold a fixed opinion, then shifting to action. He had sent the apparent smuggling fleet to Babel, drawn out the Administrator with that suicidal resistance, making him waste his time talking to Gun'gazea drawn by the lure of profit – the subsequent actions of the Cotoru D'o were no doubt caused by their own patriotism: Sei couldn't believe Mischer's strategy had gone that far – and then attack the Administration Complex while he was busy here. At that point, the "volunteer army" skillfully used SQI's biased view of pro- and anti-Administrator factions to enter the Complex, and then had their experts burrow down into SQI's innards and destroy the central core... These were the facts.

Sei fully realized that this strategy would have been totally impossible unless Mischer were accepted as one of the colonial leaders. If an Administrator had ordered the same thing, the colonists would have resisted to the death. *For us, for us colonists, for all the colonists of Gun'gazen*, so the slogans of the Independence Movement ran... Plus greed for the profit that would flow from an open Babel continent, the expectation of opening virginal Fishing Islands and Jellyfish Islands... Without a leader, the plan would have fed on itself, failed, but Mischer had been that leader. Mischer had accomplished exactly what he had said he would. Even so...

Even so, what would be the result of this temporary control of Gun'gazen? The colonists were no doubt drunk on victory, but why had Mischer, who knew the power of the Federation, and the Forces, and the Administration System, done such a thing?

Maybe it was Mischer's vanity, thought Sei. Maybe he had wanted to prove that there were leaders better than the Administrators. Well, he had proved it. Rather, it had been a fight between an Administrator inside his organization and an Administrator sunk deep into the side of the ruled. And Mischer had won. Which meant that the whole thing was just an armwrestle between two Administrators. Sei had not lost to an amateur. He had lost to an Administrator.

"New information has just come in, reported SQ2A. "A fleet of hundreds of ships has just set out from the Archipelago."

SQ2A made no other statements and drew no conclusions. That was SQ1's job. But there was no more SQ1.

Which meant...

Which meant that Sei had to do it himself. Sei understood what was happening. That was the military fleet that the United States of Gun'gazen had launched to dominate this world. Destroy the Administration Complex, occupy the islands, invade Babel, crush and enslave all Gun'gazea except those they had already befriended, take the resources, and then... Sei thought he understood what Mischer was aiming at after that. After that, they would make application for world-state independent colonial world status. They would use bribes and whatever else was needed to grasp, to gamble on that chance in a thousand. Even if it failed, Mischer would die boasting of his triumph. Maybe they would all be crushed by the Forces before they conquered this world, in which case Mischer would probably be killed by the colonists themselves.

Still...

Still... He hadn't lost completely yet, Sei said to himself. He could still...

No.

He had to discard that individualistic thinking. He was the Administrator. He couldn't allow this mud to continue to stain the authority of the System. He had to show all the colonists, all of Gun'gazea, exactly what an Administrator was.

SQ1.

Could he enter this conflict without SQ1? He could. He would.

He would personally shatter the army of the United States of Gun'gazen to splinters and dust. Maybe it was vengeance. Maybe that was not permitted to Administrators. But unless he did it there was no way to rescue the name of the Administrators, fallen into the mud. "SQ2A," he said quietly, in a low voice. His eyes hardened with resolve. "Order all robots you can communicate with to rendezvous here at once."

"But that is SQ1's authority."

"There is no SQ1."

Sei looked into the distance. "Tell them the Administrator is giving the order directly."

The fierce rain sprayed off the grass and pounded the mud. His field of vision was dark. In the darkness, Sei could hear the heavy footsteps booming ahead and behind, to the left and the right. They were the sounds of his Gun'gazea warriors, a group of warriors with a solid core of Kuwast. Their bodies encased in their traditional armor, the army plodded in silence through the pouring rain. The drenched but unstoppable army...

Sei was wet through and through. He could feel droplets of rain rolling down his almost unfeeling skin.

SQ2A, walking at Sei's side, was in the same condition. So were SQ2C, SQ2D, and SQ2E.

Since then... Since he had found out that SQ1 had been destroyed, a week had passed. In that week, they had built this united army, fought, and smashed their way through the enemy, moving forward, ever forward.

The number of robots that had responded to Sei's order to assemble, and that were now under Sei's direct command, was much smaller than he had expected.

Out of all the robots under SQ1's command, most of them were still mechanically carrying out their functions. Robots with different control frequencies were theoretically controllable, but they couldn't be contacted. On top of that, the triumphant colonists tore any single robot they found to pieces, and broadcast jamming signals, making communications between the robots much more difficult. As a result, the robots under Sei's command consisted of only SQ2A and its group, SQ2C, SQ2D, and SQ2E, and their groups. Also, as the only robots that could talk to him directly were those four high-level SQ2-class robots, he had to issue all commands through them. In addition, there was the platoon of combat robots sent by SQ1 to protect the Administrator, but they were under the control of SQ2A, and it was sufficient to deal with them through SQ2A... And that was the extent of Sei's combat strength. After he knew that, he had, without hesitation, added the Gun'gazea nation that had asked for his aid – the Kuwast. No doubt the colonists headed by Mischer had already prepared a strategy to deal with the headless army of robots, understanding its weak point. He couldn't fight with only the robots. By using the strength of the robots, and adding a thick layer of Gun'gazea warriors to the front of his lines, the colonists' plans should go awry. For that reason, he had joined with Kuwast.

The D'o of Kuwast had gladly cooperated with Sei in first smashing the Toka and the Cotoru – Sei had a reason for that too: not only were they allies of the rebels, but also they had to be punished – and then helped Sei to fight the colonists. From the viewpoint of Kuwast, if their safety could be protected with relative simplicity by the robots, then they should cooperate fully.

The united army of the robots and the Gun'gazea had set forth – north through the jungle. The awesome power of the combat robots had incredible effectiveness. After Sei's army had shattered semi-civilized Cotoru and devastated its land, they had smashed the attacking Toka grand army to the point where it could never be rebuilt. As that news filtered around, the nearby Gun'gazea responded to the ambassadors of the Kuwast and came swarming to Sei's standard, adding their strength to his.

Sei's immediate objective was the restoration of the Administration Complex – or of its ruins. After they smashed through the Toka, they turned to the northeast, and advanced soldiers towards the coast facing Unity Island.

At that time, SQ2A's attack units had reported in with information. The colonists had already landed a major force on Babel, which had left the area Sei was heading towards and proceeded to build a base camp in the hills just south of there. Considering the timing, he couldn't consider this was the main force that had set out from the Archipelago. More than likely they were from the fifty ships and the "volunteer army", coming over first on their own high spirits of victory. Sei burned. Before he grappled with the colonists' main force, it would have invaluable impact to smash their vanguard. No, more than that, they were the ones that had destroyed SQ1. He had to smash them totally, completely. Sei's army kept advancing. They advanced at full speed towards the others.

They were just entering the hilly terrain now.

The rain was lifting, slowly.

As he walked, Sei felt the weariness of his body. His body was supposed to be well-trained, but this constant walking was taking its toll after all. There was no choice but to walk. If he was to go with the Gun'gazea, he had to. That custom was deadly serious for their rites and their wars.

There was another reason Sei was tired. There was nothing at his side to take care of him, to make his meals. That had been the duty of SQ2B. SQ2B, though, had been built into the Administration Complex, and had been destroyed with SQ1. Sei had to make do with the provisions stocked in his aircraft. He could, if needed, eat the nuts and fruits here, but they tasted of heavy metals. He needed the processed food of the Administration Complex, and the plants raised hydroponically nearby… That was one reason he had to retake the Complex as soon as possible.

Strangely, though, Sei hadn't felt his helpless frustration or emptiness for a week. The situation was no longer uneasy, but had passed a climax point. Because it was behind him, now, or maybe because Sei had stopped all doubting and questioning, fixing his mind to combat… Probably for both reasons.

The rain had almost stopped now, and his range of vision increased. The landscape of grass and shrubbery began to become clearer and clearer.

"There are four kilometers remaining to the enemy camp," reported SQ2A.

"Good. Tell the robots to hold here," Sei ordered, and then called the two Kuwast D'o nearby. "Let's all rest here. During that time, I want to hold a council of war."

The D'o nodded, and called another D'o waiting nearby to relay the message to the Gun'gazea.

The SQ2-class robots relayed the command to their underlings by radio, and reported the order carried out to Sei.

The Gun'gazea were throwing up the crude war council tent now.

Just as Sei made to enter that tent, SQ2A broke in with a strange report.

"A flying object is approaching."

"A flyer?" asked Sei, turning to look at SQ2A. "Whose group?"

"It is still unclear. It is not one of my group."

"Well, then, whose is it?" SQ2C, SQ2D, and SQ2E didn't know either.

"It must be one of the remaining robots. Can't you make contact?"

"Impossible. I can't contact it on the SQ2 frequencies."

"What kind of flying object?"

"Judging from the reports received, larger than your aircraft."

"..."

Sei crooked his neck, but couldn't imagine what it might be.

At any rate, now he had to concentrate on the coming battle.

"Keep watching it," he said, and entered the tent.

By the time the council of war had ended, the rain had let up completely. The troops were aligned as the battle plan called for. The spearpoint was a group of Kuwast warriors, followed by the other Gun'gazea, including the robots. Behind them came the main force of the Kuwast, and Sei as the central main force. There was no rearguard. In that pattern, the entire army advanced. From the top of one of the hills, he could see ahead. The meandering hills, and the enemy gathered ahead. Beyond them the glittering sea and the clear outline of Unity Island...

The enemy was advancing towards them. It was a wide crescent, moving forward with magnificent control, no random movements at all.

The gap between the two armies grew smaller by the moment.

When the distance between them shrank to about five hundred meters, the enemy stopped, and Sei stopped his own forces to dress their lines.

Showdown.

He took a breath. Another. And then...

Flashing brilliantly in the sun, the flyer cut across the battlefield, flying towards Sei's central force at top speed.

"There. That is the flying object," reported SQ2A.

By then, the platoon of combat robots whose main duty was to protect the Administrator had risen up and blasted towards it.

The flyer shook off their attacks easily, and came settling down towards where Sei was standing.

"Make them stop! Make them stop this attack!" came an undoubtedly human voice from the ship's speakers.

Sei was taken aback by amazement for a moment.

A woman.

A woman's voice.

"Why don't you order them to stop?"

The voice grew sharper. "I am the Inspector. Order them to stop attacking the Inspector of the Federation!"

Inspector?

Ahh... sqi had said the Inspector was approaching Gun'gazen.

"Stop them," ordered Sei, and the combat robots stopped at once.

The flyer landed... And a woman leading a number of robots stepped out. A woman... But the real thing. A real Inspector's uniform.

Sei was still standing frozen. He had heard the Inspector was coming, and that there were women in the ranks now, but he just couldn't seem to grasp it all here, now.

"I arrived on this planet one day ago," said the Inspector. "No matter how much I radioed, there was no reception and no answer, so I investigated and found sqi destroyed. If there was no sqi, then I had to search for the Administrator alone. My robots can only communicate with the sqi of each world, so it took this much of my time."

"Oh, I see..." muttered Sei.

One of the Kuwast D'o came to his side.

"Please order the attack now."

"Stop it."

The Inspector had spoken.

"Stop this playing at war. It's over."

"I don't think that's possible," countered Sei. "To restore the authority of the Administrator, I must smash these colonists. And now they are attacking me."

The Inspector sneered a little.

"Isn't it enough to run away?"

"To... run away?"

"This kind of game is not for Administrators. For war, we have the Forces."

"Just wait one minute, " said Sei raising his palm. "I don't want solve this by borrowing the power of the Forces. This is ... this is a problem that the Administrator must deal with himself."

"It's already too late."

"What?"

"When I saw the turmoil this planet is in, I immediately issued a request for Forces assistance. They should arrive here in another five hours. They are the finest troops of Kalgeist III. These rebellious colonists will be suppressed within hours."

"You would do that?" cried Sei. Above all, he had to avoid letting this world fall into the hands of the Forces. If that happened, then what was the purpose of the Administrator System?

"Aren't you overstating your position, Sei PPKC Konda?" continued the Inspector mercilessly. "You are an Administrator. The authority of the Administrator has collapsed on this world because of you, but the Federation has countless ways to restore that authority. After the Forces have crushed these insolent colonists, we will send a new SQI and a new Administrator... The Federation can do that much without blinking an eye."

"..."

"Withdraw your troops. Let these colonists do what they like. They will all be killed by the Forces in another five hours, anyway."

Sei didn't reply.

He couldn't.

That he had failed as Administrator... that he knew. It was only natural that would be the decision.

But... what was an Administrator?

Was an Administrator really only that, only what the Inspector had said?

No. No, or at least, it hadn't always been that way. The Administrator had been necessary for the world he was in charge of. He had been needed on that world, even with those inherent contradictions... Of the two-faced god. That was how the Administrators had preserved their independence from the Federation.

It wasn't that way any more. Here on Gun'gazen, two Administrators – with Mischer, the ex-Administrator, leading the rebels – were opposed, heading for a conclusion. And now, it was all to be ended so easily by the Forces – the very same Forces that had once proved the value of the Administrator System, precisely because they were not permitted to enter the colony worlds. At the same time, the age where the Inspector had been partly the rival, and partly the partner of the Administrator was drawing to an end.

Yes...

The Administrator System was dead. The Administrator, under fire from both sides, from both the colonists and the native inhabitants, now had to withdraw from the scene. His role had ended...

Ended?

Had it really?

Was there even a single world that had achieved the basic concept of the Administrator System – to protect the colonists and raise a unified, appropriate culture for that world? To forge bonds of peace between the colonists and the native inhabitants?

That was... Sei suddenly understood. Hadn't that been nothing more than a dream from the start? When the mask had been stripped away from that dream, had fallen away – in other words, now – wouldn't the Administrator vanish and the System lose all of its meaning?

A sudden shout entered Sei's ears as he stood there.

The enemy – the rebels had begun their charge.

"Quickly, the order...!" shouted the Kuwast D'o.

"Stop it!"

The Inspector pointed at Sei. "Right now! Order them to avoid this battle and flee! Order it!"

"..."

Sei smiled. It was the first smile he had ever smiled as an Administrator – one who must never reveal his emotions. It was somehow a sad smile. Sei shook his head slowly.

"I must do it," he said. "Even if you try to strip me of my identity as Administrator... I must put an end to what I started as Administrator... It may be only foolishness to you, but that is what an Administrator is."

He faced forward, raised his right arm high, and shouted.

"Attack!"

Screaming himself, Sei ran into the center of the maelstrom of screaming warriors. In an instant, the armies crashed together, and the slaughtering ground emerged.

Sei ran forward, forward. At his side was SQ2A. And the D'o of Kuwast. Sensing it with his body and his very soul, he ran.

About the author

Mayumura Taku is the pen name of Murakami Takuji. Born in 1934, he made his first appearances in professional magazines in 1961, and has won numerous awards since. Drawing on his experiences as a "salari-man" (salaried worker) at a large manufacturer, he has written exten-sively on the depersonalization that bureaucracy forces on individuals. He is currently a professor at the Osaka University of Arts, in Osaka, Japan.

About the translator

Daniel Jackson is the pseudonym of an American-born professional translator and long-term resident of Japan. His professional interests run the gamut from technical translation to engineering. In addition to his work translating fiction, Mr. Jackson maintains several specialized web sites and conducts his own research on topics related to ancient cultures. He and his family live in a restored and renovated wood-frame home, said to be a classic of its type. Much of the available space is occupied by his large collection of English and Japanese books.

About the cover artist

Cover artist Katō Naoyuki was born in 1952; he started work as a fan artist in 1971 and made his first professional sale in 1973. His 1974 debut in *SF Magazine*, a leading Japanese science fiction monthly, initiated a string of appearances in many important publications, culminating in his receipt of the 18th Seiun Award (the Japanese Hugo) for art in 1979. He has continued to create art for *SF Magazine* and other periodicals, paper-backs (such as the Legend of Galactic Heroes series, for which he also handled mechanical design), games (most of the Traveller series), and posters, as well as a host of models based on his realistic and quasi-or-ganic designs. He has issued three cover collections in Japan, and cur-rently serves as a director of the Japanese Publication Artist League.